Praise for Ali Smith's

Autumn

"Knits together an astonishing array of seemingly disparate subjects. . . . Free spirits and the life force of art—along with kindness, hope, and a readiness 'to be above and beyond the foul even when we're up to our eyes in it'—are, when you get down to it, what Smith champions in this stirring novel." —NPR

"[A] masterwork on the post-Brexit world. . . . Impressionistic and deeply personal." —*New York*

"Smith's novel plays an intimate melody against a broader dissonance, probing the friendship between an art historian and an aging songwriter as they grapple with personal predicaments and a perilous world." —*O, The Oprah Magazine*

"Delights in puns and lyric reveries. For a book about decline and disintegration, *Autumn* remains irrepressibly hopeful about life, something 'you worked to catch, the intense happiness of an object slightly set apart from you.'" —*The Wall Street Journal*

"*Autumn* is a beautiful, poignant symphony of memories, dreams and transient realities; the 'endless sad fragility' of mortal lives."   —*The Guardian*

"In Britain, Smith has won the Whitbread, the Goldsmiths, and the Costa prizes, and has been shortlisted for the Man Booker three times. American readers ought to be better acquainted with her genius....This ambitious four-novel sequence will end with summer and Smith in her element. If we are all very lucky, perhaps the world will catch up with her there, too."   —*Slate*

"Smith regales us with endless wordplay.... *Autumn* is the first installment of Smith's 'Seasonal' quartet. If this brilliantly inventive and ruminative book is representative of what is to come, then we should welcome Smith's winter chill whatever the season."   —*Minneapolis Star Tribune*

"I find reason for excitement when Ali Smith, with thirteen titles to her credit and numerous awards and honors, brings out a new work. . . . A cycle is unfolding: winter seems to lie ahead. . . . But in inverse proportion to defeat is the great pleasure of the reading. Smith's prose is seductively simple, beguiling, its effects hard-won."
—Edward T. Wheeler, *Commonweal*

"An ambitious, multilayered creation. . . . Smith is convincing as both a twelve-year-old girl proud of her new rollerblades and a man living in a care home. . . . The story is rooted in autumn, and Smith writes lyrically about the changing seasons. . . . An energising and uplifting story."
                                        —*London Evening Standard*

"Smith is brilliant on what the referendum has done to Britain. . . . I can think of few writers— Virginia Woolf is one, James Salter another—so able to propel a narrative through voice alone. . . . This is a novel that works by accretion, appearing light and playful, surface-dwelling, while all the time enacting profound changes on the reader's heart."   —Alex Preston, *Financial Times*

"Hums with life. . . . [Smith] is indeed a writer in her prime. *Autumn* is clever and invigorating. The promise of three more books to come is something to be savored."   —*The Washington Times*

"Already acknowledged as one of the most inventive novelists writing in Britain today, with her new novel, *Autumn*, Ali Smith also proves herself to be one of the country's foremost chroniclers, her finger firmly on the social and political pulse."
                                        —*The Independent* (London)

"It is undoubtedly Smith at her best. . . . This book sets Smith's complex creative character in stone: puckish yet elegant, angry but comforting. Long may she Remain that way."

—*The Times* (London)

"Proving Smith's ambition and scope, *Autumn* is the first in a four-part series (the other titles will be *Spring*, *Winter* and *Summer*). . . . If the first installment is anything to go by, the series is destined to become a canon classic. . . . That Smith has done so with such impressive sleight of hand, and with such expediency, is incredible."

—*Irish Independent*

"Smith writes in a liltingly singsong prose that fizzes with exuberant punning and wordplay. . . . Compellingly contemporary. . . . [An] appeal to conscience and common humanity— intergenerational, interracial, international—in these deeply worrying times." —*The Irish Times*

"In bringing together the present and the seasons, Smith brings to contemporary politics the timeless injunction of art: to stop and look. . . . *Autumn* shows that the contemporary novel can be both timeless and timely. This may simply be what good novels always have done, but Smith reminds us how to do it, even now." —*Public Books*

ali smith
Autumn

Ali Smith is the author of many works of
fiction, including the novel *Hotel World*, which
was shortlisted for both the Orange Prize and
the Man Booker Prize and won the Encore
Award and the Scottish Arts Council Book of
the Year Award, and *The Accidental*, which
won the Whitbread Award and was shortlisted
for the Man Booker Prize and the Orange
Prize for Fiction. Her most recent novel, *How
to be both*, was a Man Booker Prize finalist
and winner of the Baileys Women's Prize for
Fiction, the Goldsmiths Prize, the Costa Novel
Award, and the Saltire Society Scottish Fiction
Book of the Year Award. Born in Inverness,
Scotland, Smith lives in Cambridge, England.

Autumn

ali smith
Autumn

A Novel

Anchor Books
A Division of Penguin Random House LLC
New York

FIRST ANCHOR BOOKS EDITION, OCTOBER 2017

Copyright © 2016 by Ali Smith

All rights reserved. Published in the United States by Anchor Books, a division of Penguin Random House LLC, New York. Originally published in hardcover in Great Britain by Hamish Hamilton, an imprint of Penguin Books Ltd., a division of Penguin Random House Ltd., London, in 2016, and subsequently published in hardcover in the United States by Pantheon Books, a division of Penguin Random House LLC, New York, in 2017.

Anchor Books and colophon are registered trademarks of Penguin Random House LLC.

Grateful acknowledgment is made to the following for permission to reprint previously published material: Pan Books: Excerpt from *Talking to Women* by Nell Dunn, copyright © 1966 by Nell Dunn. Reprinted by permission of Pan Books. Penguin Books Ltd.: Excerpt from *Metamorphoses* by Ovid, translated by Mary M. Innes. Copyright © 1995 by Mary M. Innes. Reprinted by permission of Penguin Books Ltd. Wolverhampton Art Gallery & Museums: Excerpt from *Pauline Boty: Pop Artist and Woman* by Sue Tate, copyright © 2013 by Sue Tate. Reprinted by permission of Wolverhampton Art Gallery & Museums.

The Library of Congress has cataloged the Pantheon edition as follows:
Name: Smith, Ali, [date] author.
Title: Autumn / Ali Smith.
Description: New York : Pantheon Books, [2017]
Identifiers: LCCN 2016036972 (print). LCCN 2016044805 (ebook).
Subjects: BISAC: FICTION / Literary. FICTION / Visionary & Metaphysical. FICTION / Contemporary Women.
Classification: LCC PR6069.M4213 A92 2017 (print).
LCC PR6069.M4213 (e-book).
DDC823/.914—dc23
LC record available at lccn.loc.gov/2016036972

Anchor Books Trade Paperback ISBN: 978-1-101-96994-6
eBook ISBN: 978-1-101-87074-7

www.anchorbooks.com

Printed in the United States of America
10 9 8 7 6

For Gilli Bush-Bailey
see you next week

and for Sarah Margaret
Hardy perennial Wood

Spring come to you at the farthest,
In the very end of harvest!
William Shakespeare

At current rates of soil erosion, Britain has just
100 harvests left.
Guardian, 20 July 2016

Green as the grass we lay in corn, in sunlight
Ossie Clark

If I am destined to be happy with you here –
how short is the longest Life.
John Keats

Gently disintegrate me
WS Graham

1

It was the worst of times, it was the worst of times.
Again. That's the thing about things. They fall apart,
always have, always will, it's in their nature. So an
old old man washes up on a shore. He looks like a
punctured football with its stitching split, the leather
kind that people kicked a hundred years ago. The
sea's been rough. It has taken the shirt off his back;
naked as the day I was born are the words in the head
he moves on its neck, but it hurts to. So try not to
move the head. What's this in his mouth, grit? it's
sand, it's under his tongue, he can feel it, he can hear it
grinding when his teeth move against each other,
singing its sand-song: I'm ground so small, but in the
end I'm all, I'm softer if I'm underneath you when you
fall, in sun I glitter, wind heaps me over litter, put a
message in a bottle, throw the bottle in the sea, the
bottle's made of me, I'm the hardest grain to harvest

3

to harvest

the words for the song trickle away. He is tired. The sand in his mouth and his eyes is the last of the grains in the neck of the sandglass.

Daniel Gluck, your luck's run out at last.

He prises open one stuck eye. But —

Daniel sits up on the sand and the stones

— is this it? really? this? is death?

He shades his eyes. Very bright.

Sunlit. Terribly cold, though.

He is on a sandy stony strand, the wind distinctly harsh, the sun out, yes, but no heat off it. Naked, too. No wonder he's cold. He looks down and sees that his body's still the old body, the ruined knees.

He'd imagined death would distil a person, strip the rotting rot away till everything was light as a cloud.

Seems the self you get left with on the shore, in the end, is the self that you were when you went.

If I'd known, Daniel thinks, I'd have made sure to go at twenty, twenty five.

Only the good.

Or perhaps (he thinks, one hand shielding his face so if anyone can see him no one will be offended by him picking out what's in the lining of his nose, or giving it a look to see what it is — it's sand, beautiful the detail, the different array of colours of even the pulverized world, then he rubs it away off his fingertips) this *is* my self distilled. If so then death's a sorry disappointment.

Thank you for having me, death. Please excuse me, must get back to it, life.

He stands up. It doesn't hurt, not so much, to. Now then.

Home. Which way?

He turns a half circle. Sea, shoreline, sand, stones. Tall grass, dunes. Flatland behind the dunes. Trees past the flatland, a line of woods, all the way back round to the sea again.

The sea is strange and calm.

Then it strikes him how unusually good his eyes are today.

I mean, I can see not just those woods, I can see not just that tree, I can see not just that leaf on that tree. I can see the stem connecting that leaf to that tree.

He can focus on the loaded seedhead at the end of any piece of grass on those dunes over there pretty much as if he were using a camera zoom. And did he just look down at his own hand and see not just his hand, in focus, and not just a scuff of sand on the side of his hand, but several separate grains of sand so clearly delineated that he can see their edges, and (hand goes to his forehead) *no glasses*?

Well.

He rubs sand off his legs and arms and chest then

off his hands. He watches the flight of the grains of it as it dusts away from him in the air. He reaches down, fills his hand with sand. Look at that. So many.

Chorus:
How many worlds can you hold in a hand.
In a handful of sand.
(Repeat.)

He opens his fingers. The sand drifts down.

Now that he's up on his feet he is hungry. Can you be hungry *and* dead? Course you can, all those hungry ghosts eating people's hearts and minds. He turns the full circle back to the sea. He hasn't been on a boat for more than fifty years, and that wasn't really a boat, it was a terrible novelty bar, party place on the river. He sits down on the sand and stones again but the bones are hurting in his, he doesn't want to use impolite language, there's a girl there further up the shore, are hurting like, he doesn't want to use impolite –

A girl?

Yes, with a ring of girls round her, all doing a wavy ancient Greek looking dance. The girls are quite close. They're coming closer.

This won't do. The nakedness.

Then he looks down again with his new eyes at where his old body was a moment ago and he knows he is dead, he must be dead, he is surely dead, because his body looks different from the last time he looked down at it, it looks better, it looks rather good as bodies go. It looks very familiar, very like his own body but back when it was young.

A girl is nearby. Girls. Sweet deep panic and shame flood through him.

He makes a dash for the long grass dunes (he can run, really run!), he puts his head round the side of a grass tuft to check nobody can see him, nobody coming, and up and off (again! not even breathless) across the flatland towards those woods.

There will be cover in the woods.

There will maybe be something too with which to cover himself up. But pure joy! He'd forgotten what it feels like, to feel. To feel even just the thought of one's own bared self near someone else's beauty.

There's a little copse of trees. He slips into the copse. Perfect, the ground in the shade, carpeted with leaves, the fallen leaves under his (handsome, young) feet are dry and firm, and on the lower branches of the trees too a wealth of leaves still bright green, and look, the hair on his body is dark black again all up his arms, and from his chest down to the groin where it's thick, ah, not just the hair, everything is thickening, look.

This is heaven all right.

Above all, he doesn't want to offend.

He can make a bed here. He can stay here while he gets his bearings. Bare-ings. (Puns, the poor man's currency; poor old John Keats, well, poor all right, though you couldn't exactly call him old. Autumn poet, winter Italy, days away from dying he found himself punning like there was no tomorrow. Poor chap. There really was no tomorrow.) He can heap these leaves up over himself to keep him warm at night, if there's such a thing as night when you're dead, and if that girl, those girls, come any closer he'll heap a yard of them over his whole self so as not to dishonour.

Decent.

He had forgotten there is a physicality in not wanting to offend. Sweet the feeling of decency flooding him now, surprisingly like you imagine it would be to drink nectar. The beak of the hummingbird entering the corolla. That rich. That sweet. What rhymes with nectar? He will make a green suit for himself out of leaves, and – as soon as he thinks it, a needle and some kind of gold coloured threading stuff on a little bobbin appears here in his hand, look. He *is* dead. He must be. It is perhaps rather fine, after all, being dead. Highly underrated in the modern western world. Someone should tell them. Someone should let them know. Someone should be sent, scramble back to, wherever it is. Recollect her. Affect her. Neglect her. Lie detector. Film projector. Director. Collector. Objector.

He picks a green leaf off the branch by his head.

He picks another. He puts their edges together. He
stitches one to the other with a neat, what is it,
running stitch? blanket stitch? Look at that. He can
sew. Not something he could do while he was alive.
Death. Full of surprises. He picks up a layering of
leaves. He sits down, matches an edge to an edge
and sews. Remember that postcard he bought off a
rack in the middle of Paris in the 1980s, of the little
girl in one of the parks? She looked like she was
dressed in dead leaves, black and white photo
dated not long after the war ended, the child from
behind, dressed in the leaves, standing in the park
looking at scattered leaves and trees ahead of her.
But it was a tragic as well as a fetching picture.
Something about the child plus the dead leaves,
terrible anomaly, a bit like she was wearing rags.
Then again, the rags weren't rags. They were
leaves, so it was a picture about magic and
transformation too. But then again *again*, a picture
taken not long after, in a time when a child just
playing in leaves could look, for the first time to
the casual eye, like a rounded-up and offed child
(it hurts to think it)
    or maybe also a nuclear after-child, the leaves
hanging off her looked like skin become rags,
hanging to one side as if skin *is* nothing but leaves.
    So it was fetching in the other sense of fetch too,
the picture, like a picture of your *fetch*, the one who
comes to fetch you off to the other world. One

blink of a camera eye (can't quite put his finger on the name of the photographer) and that child dressed in leaves became all these things: sad, terrible, beautiful, funny, terrifying, dark, light, charming, fairystory, folkstory, truth. The more mundane truth was, he'd bought that postcard (Boubat! *he* took it) when he visited the city of love with yet another woman he wanted to love him but she didn't, course she didn't, a woman in her forties, a man in his late sixties, well, be honest, nearer seventy, and anyway he didn't love her either. Not truly. Matter of profound mismatch nothing to do with age, since at the Pompidou Centre he'd been so moved by the wildness in a painting by Dubuffet that he'd taken his shoes off and knelt down in front of it to show respect, and the woman, her name was Sophie something, had been embarrassed and in the taxi to the airport told him he was too old to take off his shoes in an art gallery, even a modern one.

In fact all he can remember of her is that he sent her a postcard he wished afterwards he'd kept for himself.

He wrote on the back of it, *with love from an old child*.

He is always looking out for that picture.

He has never found it again.

He has always regretted not keeping it.

Regrets when you're dead? A past when you're

dead? Is there never any escaping the junkshop of the self?

He looks out from the copse at the edge of the land, the sea.

Well, wherever it is I've ended, it's given me this very swanky green coat.

He wraps it around him. It's a good fit, it smells leafy and fresh. He would make a good tailor. He has made something, made something of himself. His mother would be pleased at last.

Oh God. Is there still mother after death?

He is a boy collecting chestnuts from the ground under the trees. He splits the bright green prickly cauls and frees them brown and shining from the waxy pith. He fills his cap with them. He takes them to his mother. She is over here with the new baby.

Don't be stupid, Daniel. She can't eat these. Nothing eats these, not even horses, far too bitter.

Daniel Gluck, seven years old, in good clothes he's always being told how lucky he is to have in a world where so many have so little, looks down at the conkers he should never have sullied his good cap with and sees the brown shine on them go dull.

Bitter memories, even when you're dead.

How very disheartening.

Never mind. Hearten up.

He's on his feet. He is his respectable self again. He scouts around him, finds some large rocks and a

11

couple of good-sized sticks with which he marks the door of his copse so he'll find it again.

In his bright green coat he comes out of the woods, across the plain and back towards the shore.

But the sea? Silent, like sea in a dream.

The girl? No sign. The ring of dancers round her? Gone. On the shore, though, there's a washed-up body. He goes to look. Is it his own?

No. It is a dead person.

Just along from this dead person, there is another dead person. Beyond it, another, and another.

He looks along the shore at the dark line of the tide-dumped dead.

Some of the bodies are of very small children. He crouches down near a swollen man who has a child, just a baby really, still zipped inside his jacket, its mouth open, dripping sea, its head resting dead on the bloated man's chest.

Further up the beach there are more people. These people are human, like the ones on the shore, but these are alive. They're under parasols. They are holidaying up the shore from the dead.

There is music coming out of a screen. One of the people is working on a computer. Another is sitting in the shade reading a little screen. Another is dozing under the same parasol, another is rubbing suncream into his shoulder and down his arm.

A child squealing with laughter is running in and out of the water, dodging the bigger waves.

Daniel Gluck looks from the death to the life, then back to the death again.

The world's sadness.

Definitely still in the world.

He looks down at his leaf coat, still green.

He holds out a forearm, still miraculous, young.

It will not last, the dream.

He takes hold of one leaf at the corner of his coat. He holds it hard. He will take it back with him if he can. Proof of where he's been.

What else can he bring?

How did that chorus go, again?

How many worlds

Handful of sand

It is a Wednesday, just past midsummer. Elisabeth
Demand – thirty two years old, no-fixed-hours
casual contract junior lecturer at a university in
London, living the dream, her mother says, and she
is, if the dream means having no job security and
almost everything being too expensive to do and
that you're still in the same rented flat you had
when you were a student over a decade ago – has
gone to the main Post Office in the town nearest the
village her mother now lives in, to do Check &
Send with her passport form.

Apparently this service makes things quicker. It
means your passport can be issued in half the time,
if you've gone in with your form filled out and with
your old passport and your new photographs, and
had a certified Post Office official check it through
with you before it goes to the Passport Office.

The Post Office ticket machine gives her a ticket with number 233 on it for counter service. The place isn't busy, apart from the queue of angry people stretching out the door for the self-service weighing machines, for which there's no ticketing system. But the number she's been given is so far ahead of the numbers highlighted on the boards above everybody's heads as *coming up next* (156, 157, 158), and it takes so long anyway for the lone two people behind the twelve counters to serve the people who are presumably numbers 154 and 155 (she's been here twenty minutes and they're still the same two customers) that she leaves the Post Office, crosses the green, goes to the second-hand bookshop on Bernard Street.

When she gets back ten minutes later the same two lone people behind the counters are still the only people serving. But the screen now says that the numbers *coming up next* for counter service will be 284, 285 and 286.

Elisabeth presses the button on the machine and takes another ticket (365). She sits down on the circular communal seating unit in the middle of the room. Something inside it is broken, so that when she does this something clanks inside its structure and the person sitting along from her is jerked an inch into the air. Then that person shifts position, the seat clanks again and Elisabeth jolts an inch or so downwards.

Through the windows, there on the other side of the road, she can see the grand municipal building that used to be the town Post Office. It's now a row of designer chainstores. Perfume. Clothes. Cosmetics. She looks round the room again. The people sitting on the communal seat are almost all exactly the same people who were here when she first came in. She opens the book in her hand. Brave New World. Chapter One. *A squat grey building of only thirty-four storeys. Over the main entrance the words, CENTRAL LONDON HATCHERY AND CONDITIONING CENTRE, and, in a shield, the World State's motto, COMMUNITY, IDENTITY, STABILITY.* An hour and forty five minutes later, when she's quite far through the book, most of the people round her are still those same people. They're still staring into space. They occasionally clank the chair. Nobody talks to anyone else. Nobody has said a single word to her the whole time she's been here. The only thing that changes is the queue snaking towards the self-service weighing machines. Occasionally someone crosses the room to look at the commemorative coins in the plastic display unit. There's a set, she can see from here, for Shakespeare's birthday or deathday anniversary. There's a skull on one of the coins. Presumably deathday, then.

Elisabeth goes back to the book and by chance

the page she's on happens to be quoting Shakespeare. *'O brave new world!' Miranda was proclaiming the possibility of loveliness, the possibility of transforming even the nightmare into something fine and noble. 'O brave new world!' It was a challenge, a command.* To look up from it and see the commemorative money at the very second when the book brings Shakespeare and itself properly together – that's really something. She shifts in her seat and clanks the chair by mistake. The woman along from her jumps slightly in the air but gives no sign at all that she knows or cares that she has.

It's funny to be sitting on such an uncommunal communal chair.

There's no one Elisabeth can exchange a look with about that, though, let alone tell the thing she's just thought about the book and the coins.

In any case, it's one of those coincidences that on TV and in books might mean something but in real life mean nothing at all. What would they put on a commemorative coin to celebrate Shakespeare's *birth*day? O brave new world. That'd be good. That's a bit like what it's like, presumably, to be born. If anyone could ever remember being born.

The board says 334.

Hello, Elisabeth says to the man behind the counter forty or so minutes later.

The number of days in the year, the man says.

I'm sorry? Elisabeth says.

Number 365, the man says.

I've read nearly a whole book while I've been waiting here this morning, Elisabeth says. And it struck me that maybe it'd be a good idea to have books available here so all the people who end up waiting could have a read too, if they'd like to. Have you ever thought of opening or installing a small library?

Funny you should say that, the man says. Most of those people aren't here for Post Office services at all. Since the library closed this is where they come if it's raining or intemperate.

Elisabeth looks back at where she was sitting. The seat she's just left has been taken by a very young woman breastfeeding a baby.

Anyway, thank you for your query, and I hope we've answered it to your full satisfaction, the man is saying.

He is about to press the button next to him to call 366 to the counter.

No! Elisabeth says.

The man creases up. It seems he was joking; his shoulders go up and down but no sound comes out of him. It's like laughter, but also like a parody of laughter, and simultaneously a bit like he's having an asthma attack. Maybe you're not allowed to laugh out loud behind the counter of the main Post Office.

I'm only here once a week, Elisabeth says. I'd

have had to come back next week if you'd
done that.

The man glances at her Check & Send form.

And you may well have to come back next week
anyway, he says. It's a nine times out of ten-er that
something's not going to be right with this.

Very funny, Elisabeth says.

I'm not joking, the man says. You can't joke
about passports.

The man empties all the papers out of her
envelope on his side of the divide.

I just have to make it clear to you first up before
we check anything, he says, that if I go ahead now
and check your Check & Send form today it'll cost
you £9.75. I mean £9.75 today. And if by chance
something isn't correct in it today, it'll still cost you
£9.75 today, and you'll need to pay me that money
anyway even if we can't send it off because of
whatever incorrect thing.

Right, Elisabeth says.

But. Having said that, the man says. If something's
not correct and you pay the £9.75 today, which you
have to do, and you correct the thing that's not
correct and bring it back here within one month,
provided you can show your receipt, then you won't
be charged another £9.75. However. If you bring it
back *after* one month, or *without* your receipt,
you'll be charged another £9.75 for another
Check & Send service.

Got it, Elisabeth says.

Are you sure you still want to go ahead with today's Check & Send? the man says.

Uh huh, Elisabeth says.

Could you say the word yes, rather than just make that vaguely affirmative sound you're making, please, the man says.

Uh, Elisabeth says. Yes.

Though you'll have to pay even if the Check & Send isn't successful today?

I'm beginning to hope it won't be, Elisabeth says. There's a few old classics I haven't read yet.

Think you're funny? the man says. Would you like me to fetch you a complaints form and you can fill it in while you wait? If you do, though, I have to advise you that you'll need to leave the counter while I serve someone else and because I'm shortly due my lunch break you'll lose your consecutive place and will have to take a new counter service ticket from the machine and wait your turn.

I've absolutely no wish to complain about anything, Elisabeth says.

The man is looking at her filled-in form.

Is your surname really Demand? he says.

Uh huh, Elisabeth says. I mean yes.

A name you live up to, he says. As we've already ascertained.

Uh, Elisabeth says.

Only joking, the man says.

21

His shoulders go up and down.

And you're sure you've spelt your Christian name correctly? he says.

Yes, Elisabeth says.

That's not the normal way of spelling it, the man says. The normal way of spelling it is with a z. As far as I'm aware.

Mine is with an s, Elisabeth says.

Fancy way, the man says.

It's my name, Elisabeth says.

It's people from other countries that spell it like that, generally, isn't it? the man says.

He flicks through the outdated passport.

But this does say you're UK, he says.

I am, Elisabeth says.

Same spelling in here, the s and all, he says.

Amazingly, Elisabeth says.

Don't be sarky, the man says.

Now he's comparing the photograph inside the old passport with the new sheet of booth shots Elisabeth has brought with her.

Recognizable, he says. Just. (Shoulders.) And that's just the change from twenty two to thirty two. Wait till you see the difference when you come back in here for a new passport in ten years' time. (Shoulders.)

He checks the numbers she's written on the form against the ones in the outdated passport.

Going travelling? he says.

Probably, Elisabeth says. Just in case.

Where you thinking of going? he says.

Lots of places, I expect, Elisabeth says. Who knows? World. Oyster.

Seriously allergic, the man says. Don't even say the word. If I die this afternoon, I'll know who to tell them to blame.

Shoulders. Up, down.

Then he puts the booth photographs down in front of him. He screws his mouth over to one side. He shakes his head.

What? Elisabeth says.

No, I think it's all right, he says. The hair. It has to be completely clear of your eyes.

It *is* completely clear of my eyes, Elisabeth says. It's nowhere near my eyes.

It also can't be anywhere near your face, the man says.

It's on my head, Elisabeth says. That's where it grows. And my face is also attached to my head.

Witticism, the man says, will make not a jot of difference to the stipulations which mean you can, in the end, be issued a passport, which you will need before you are permitted to go anywhere not in this island realm. In other words. Will get you. Nowhere.

Right, Elisabeth says. Thanks.

I think it's all right, the man says.

Good, Elisabeth says.

Wait, the man says. Wait a minute. Just a.

He gets up off his chair and ducks down behind the divide. He comes back up with a cardboard box. In it are various pairs of scissors, rubbers, a stapler, paperclips and a rolled-up measuring tape. He takes the tape in his hands and unrolls the first centimetres of it. He places the tape against one of the images of Elisabeth on the booth sheet.

Yes, he says.

Yes? Elisabeth says.

I thought so, he says. 24 millimetres. As I thought.

Good, Elisabeth says.

Not good, the man says. I'm afraid not good at all. Your face is the wrong size.

How can my face be a wrong size? Elisabeth says.

You didn't follow the instructions about filling the facial frame, that's if the photobooth you used is fitted with passport instructions, the man says. Of course, it's possible the booth you used wasn't passport-instruction-fitted. But that doesn't help here either way I'm afraid.

What size is my face meant to be? Elisabeth says.

The correct size for a face in the photograph submitted, the man says, is between 29 millimetres and 34 millimetres. Yours falls short by 5 millimetres.

Why does my face need to be a certain size? Elisabeth says.

Because it's what is stipulated, the man says.

Is it for facial recognition technology? Elisabeth says.

The man looks her full in the face for the
first time.

Obviously I can't process the form without the
correct stipulation, he says.

He takes a piece of paper off a pile to the right
of him.

You should go to Snappy Snaps, he says as he
stamps a little circle on the piece of paper with a
metal stamp. They'll do it there for you to the
correct specification. Where are you planning to
travel to?

Well, nowhere, till I get the new passport,
Elisabeth says.

He points to the unstamped circle next to the
stamped one.

If you bring it back within a month of this date,
provided everything's correct, you won't have to pay
£9.75 for another Check & Send, he says. Where did
you say you were thinking of going, again?

I didn't, Elisabeth says.

Hope you won't take it the wrong way if I write
in this box that you're wrong in the head, the
man says.

His shoulders aren't moving. He writes in a box next
to the word *Other*: HEAD INCORRECT SIZE.

If this were a drama on TV, Elisabeth says, you
know what would happen now?

It's largely rubbish, TV, the man says. I prefer
box sets.

What I'm saying is, Elisabeth says, in the next shot you'd be dead of oyster poisoning and I'd be being arrested and blamed for something I didn't do.

Power of suggestion, the man says.

Suggestion of power, Elisabeth says.

Oh, very clever, the man says.

And also, this notion that my head's the wrong size in a photograph would mean I've probably done or am going to do something really wrong and illegal, Elisabeth says. And because I asked you about facial recognition technology, because I happen to know it exists and I asked you if the passport people use it, that makes me a suspect as well. And there's the notion, too, in your particular take on our story so far, that I might be some kind of weirdo because there's an s in my name instead of a z.

I'm sorry? the man says.

Like if a child cycles past in a drama or a film, Elisabeth says, like the way if you're watching a film or a drama and there's a child cycling away on a bicycle and you see the child going, getting further away, and especially if you watch this happen from a camera position behind that child, well, something terrible's bound to be about to happen to that child, for sure it'll be the last time you'll see that child, that child still innocent, anyway. You can't just be a child and cycle away because you're off to the shops any more. Or if there's a happy man or woman driving a car, just out driving, enjoying it, nothing else happening – and especially if this is edited into someone else's waiting for that person to come home – then he or she is probably definitely about to crash and die. Or, if it's a woman, to be abducted and come to a gruesome sex-crime end, or to disappear. Probably definitely he or she one way or another is driving to his or her doom.

The man folds the Check & Send receipt and tucks it into the envelope Elisabeth gave him with the form, the old passport and the unsuitable photographs. He hands it back to her across the divide. She sees terrible despondency in his eyes. He sees her see it. He hardens even more. He opens a drawer, takes a laminated sheet out of it and places it at the front of the divide.

Position Closed.

This isn't fiction, the man says. This is the Post Office.

Elisabeth watches him go through the swing door at the back.

She pushes her way through the self-service queue and out of the non-fictional Post Office.

She crosses the green to the bus station.

She's going to The Maltings Care Providers plc to see Daniel.

Daniel is still here.

The last three times Elisabeth's been, he's been asleep. He'll be asleep this time too, when she gets there. She'll sit on the chair next to the bed and get the book out of her bag.

Brave old world.

Daniel will be so asleep that he'll look like he's never going to wake up.

Hello Mr Gluck, she'll say if he does. Sorry I'm late. I was having my face measured and rejected for being the wrong specification.

But there's no point in thinking this. He won't.

If he were to wake, the first thing he'd do is he'd tell her some fact from whichever fruitful place in his brain he'd been down deep in.

Oh a long queue of them, Daniel'd say, all the

way up the mountain. A line of tramps from the foot to the peak of one of the Sacramento mountains.

Sounds serious, she'd say.

It was, he'd say. Nothing comic isn't serious. And he was the greatest comedian of all. He hired them, hundreds and hundreds of them, and they were real, the real thing, real tramps to his movie star tramp, real loners, real lost and homeless men. He wanted it to look like the real gold rush. The local police said the tramps weren't to be paid any money by the producers till they'd all been rounded up and taken back to Sacramento City. They didn't want them going all over the district. And when he was a boy – the boy who ended life as one of the richest, the most famous men in the world – when he was a boy in the poorhouse for children, the orphanage, when his mother was taken to the asylum, he got given a bag of sweets and an orange at Christmas time, all the kids in the place got the same. But the difference, here's the difference. He made that December bag of sweets last all the way to October.

He'd shake his head.

Genius, he'd say.

Then he'd squint at Elisabeth.

Oh, hello, he'd say.

He'd look at the book in her hands.

What you reading? he'd say.
Elisabeth would hold it up.
Brave New World, she'd say.
Oh, that old thing, he'd say.
It's new to me, she'd say.

That moment of dialogue? Imagined.

Daniel is now in an increased sleep period. Whichever care assistant chances to be on duty always makes a point of explaining, when Elisabeth sits with him, that the increased sleep period happens when people are close to death.

He is beautiful.

He is so tiny in the bed. It is like he is just a head. He's small and frail now, thin as the skeleton of a cartoon fish left by a cartoon cat, his body so near-nothing under the covers that it hardly makes any impression, just a head by itself on a pillow, a head with a cave in it and the cave is his mouth.

His eyes are closed and watery. There's a long time between each breath in and out. In that long time there's no breathing at all, so that every time he breathes out there's the possibility that he might not breathe in again, it doesn't seem quite possible that someone could be able not to breathe for so long and yet still be breathing and alive.

A good old age, he's done very well, the care assistants say.

He's had a good innings, the care assistants say, as if to say, it won't be long now.

Oh really?

They don't know Daniel.

Are you next of kin? Because we've been trying to contact Mr Gluck's next of kin with no success, the receptionist said the first time Elisabeth came. Elisabeth lied without even pausing. She gave them her mobile number, her mother's home number and her mother's home address.

We'll need further proof of identity, the receptionist said.

Elisabeth got out her passport.

I'm afraid this passport has expired, the receptionist said.

Yes, but only a month ago. I'm going to renew it. It's obviously still clearly me, Elisabeth said.

The receptionist started a speech about what was and what wasn't permitted. Then something happened at the front door, a wheelchair wheel jammed in a groove between the ramp and the edge of the door, and the receptionist went to find someone to free the wheelchair up. An assistant came through from the back. This assistant, seeing

Elisabeth putting her passport back into her bag, assumed that the passport had been checked and printed out a visitor card for Elisabeth.

Now, when Elisabeth sees the man whose wheelchair wheel got caught in the groove, she smiles at him. He looks back at her like he doesn't know who she is. Well, it's true. He doesn't.

She brings a chair in from the corridor and puts it next to the bed.

Then, in case Daniel opens his eyes (he dislikes attention), she gets out whatever book she's got with her.

With the book open in her hands, Brave New World, she looks at the top of his head. She looks at the darker spots in the skin beneath what's left of his hair.

Daniel, as still as death in the bed. But still. He's still here.

Elisabeth, at a loss, gets her phone out. She keys in the word *still* on her phone, just to see what'll come up.

The internet provides her instantly with a series of sentences to show usage of the word.

How still everything was!
She still held Jonathan's hand.
When they turned around, Alex was still
*   on the horse.*
Still, it did look stylish.

The throng stood still and waited.
Then Psammetichus tried still another plan.
When he still didn't respond, she continued.
People were still alive who knew the Wright
    Brothers.

Ah yes, Orville and Will, the two flighty boys
who started it all, Daniel, lying there so still, says
without saying. The boys who gave us the world in
a day, and air warfare, and every bored and restless
security queue in the world. But I will lay you a
wager (he says/doesn't say) that they don't have the
kind of *still* on that list which forms part of the
word di*still*ery.

Elisabeth scrolls down to check.

And that word scroll, Daniel says without saying,
it makes me think of all the scrolls still rolled up,
unread for two millennia, still waiting to be
unfurled in the still-unexcavated library in
Herculaneum.

She scrolls to the bottom of the page.

You're right, Mr Gluck. No whisky still.

Still, Daniel says/doesn't say. I *do* look stylish.

Daniel lies there very still in the bed, and the cave
of his mouth, its unsaying of these things, is the
threshold to the end of the world as she knows it.

Elisabeth is staring up at an old tenement rooming house, the kind you see being bulldozed and crashing down into themselves on old footage from when they modernized British cities in the 1960s and 70s.

It is still standing, but in a ravaged landscape. All the other houses have been pulled out of the street like bad teeth.

She pushes the door open. Its hall is dark, its wallpaper stained and dark. The front room is empty, no furniture. Its floor has boards broken where whoever was living or squatting here ripped them up to burn in the hearth, above the old mantel of which a shock of soot-grime shoots almost to the ceiling.

She imagines its walls white. She imagines everything in it painted white.

Even the holes in the floor, through the white broken boards, are painted white inside.

The house's windows look out on to high privet hedge. Elisabeth goes outside to paint that high hedge white too.

Inside, sitting on a white-painted old couch, the stuffing coming out of it also stiff with white emulsion, Daniel laughs at what she's doing. He laughs silently but like a child with his feet in his hands as she paints one tiny green leaf white after another.

He catches her eye. He winks. That does it.

They're both standing in pure clean white space.

Yes, she says. Now we can sell this space for a fortune. Only the very rich can afford to be this minimalist these days.

Daniel shrugs. Plus ça change.

Will we go for a walk, Mr Gluck? Elisabeth says.

But Daniel's off on his own already, crossing the white desert at a fair rate. She tries to catch him up. She can't quite. He's always just too far ahead. The whiteness goes on forever ahead of them. When she looks over her shoulder it's forever behind them too.

Someone killed an MP, she tells Daniel's back as she struggles to keep up. A man shot her dead and came at her with a knife. Like shooting her wouldn't be enough. But it's old news now. Once it would have been a year's worth of news. But news right now is like a flock of speeded-up sheep running off the side of a cliff.

The back of Daniel's head nods.

Thomas Hardy on speed, Elisabeth says.

Daniel stops and turns. He smiles benignly.

His eyes are closed. He breathes in. He breathes out. He is dressed in clothes made of hospital sheets. They've got the hospital name stamped on the corners, occasionally she can see it, pink and blue writing on a cuff or at the corner in the lining at the bottom of the jacket. He is peeling a white orange with a white penknife. The scroll of peel falls into the whiteness like into deep snow and disappears. He watches this happen and he makes an annoyed noise, tch. He looks at the peeled orange in his hand. It's white. He shakes his head.

He pats his pockets, chest, trousers, as if he's looking for something. Then he pulls, straight out of his chest, of his collarbone, like a magician, a free-floating mass of the colour orange.

He throws it like a huge cloak over the whiteness ahead of them. Before it settles away from him he twists a little of it round a finger and binds it round the too-white orange he's still holding.

The white orange in his hand becomes its natural colour.

He nods.

He pulls the colours green and blue like a string of handkerchiefs out of the centre of himself. The orange in his hand turns Cézanne-colours.

People crowd round him, excited.

People queue up, bring him their white things, hold them out.

Anonymous people start to add tweet-sized comments about Daniel beneath Daniel. They are commenting on his ability to change things.

The comments get more and more unpleasant.

They start to make a sound like a hornet mass and Elisabeth notices that what looks like liquid excrement is spreading very close to her bare feet. She tries not to step in any of it.

She calls to Daniel to watch where he steps too.

Having a bit of time out? the care assistant says. All
right for some, huh?

Elisabeth comes to, opens her eyes. The book
falls off her lap. She picks it up.

The care assistant is tapping the rehydration bag.

Some of us have to work for a living, she says.

She winks in the general direction of Elisabeth.

I was miles away, Elisabeth says.

Him too, the care assistant says. A very nice
polite gentleman. We miss him now. Increased sleep
period. It happens when things are becoming more
(slight pause before she says it) final.

The pauses are a precise language, more a
language than actual language is, Elisabeth thinks.

Please don't talk about Mr Gluck as if he can't
hear you, she says. He can hear you as well as I can.
Even if it looks like he's asleep.

The care assistant hooks the chart she's been looking at back on the rail at the end of the bed.

One day I was giving him a wash, she says as if Elisabeth's not there either and as if she's quite used to people not being there, or equally to having to function as if people aren't.

And the TV was on in the lounge, loud, and his door was open. He opens his eyes and sits straight up in the bed in the middle of. Advert, a supermarket. A song starts above the people's heads in the shop and all the people buying the things, dropping them on the floor instead and are dancing everywhere in the shop, and he sat straight up in the bed, he said this one is me, I wrote this one.

Old queen, Elisabeth's mother said under her breath.

Why him? she said at the more normal level of voice.

Because he's our neighbour, Elisabeth said.

It was a Tuesday evening in April in 1993. Elisabeth was eight years old.

But we don't know him, her mother said.

We're supposed to talk to a neighbour about what it means to be a neighbour, then make a portrait in words of a neighbour, Elisabeth said. You're meant to come with me, I'm meant to make up two or three questions and ask them to a neighbour for the portrait and you're meant to accompany me. I *told* you. I told you on Friday. You said we would. It's for school.

Her mother was doing something to the make-up on her eyes.

43

About what? her mother said. About all the arty art he's got in there?

We've got pictures, Elisabeth said. Are they arty art?

She looked at the wall behind her mother, the picture of the river and the little house. The picture of the squirrels made from bits of real pinecone. The poster of the dancers by Henri Matisse. The poster of the woman and her skirt and the Eiffel Tower. The blown-up real photographs of her grandmother and grandfather from when her mother was small. The ones of her mother when her mother was a baby. The ones of herself as a baby.

The stone with the hole through the middle of it. In the middle of his front room, her mother was saying. That's very arty art. I wasn't being nosy. I was passing. The light was on. I thought you were supposed to be collecting and identifying fallen leaves.

That was like three weeks ago, Elisabeth said. Are you going out?

Can't we phone Abbie and ask her the questions over the phone? her mother said.

But we don't live next to Abbie any more, Elisabeth said. It's supposed to be someone who's a neighbour *right now*. It's supposed to be in person, an in-person interview. And I'm supposed to ask about what it was like where the neighbour grew up

and what life was like when the neighbour was
my age.

People's lives are private, her mother said. You
can't just go traipsing into their lives asking all sorts
of questions. And anyway. Why does the school
want to know these things about our neighbours?

They just do, Elisabeth said.

She went and sat on the top step of the stairs.
She'd end up being the new girl who hasn't done the
right homework. Her mother was going to say any
minute now that she was off to do shopping at the
late-night Tesco's and that she'd be back in half an
hour. In reality she'd be back in two hours. She
would smell of cigarettes. There'd be nothing
brought back from Tesco's.

It's about history, and being neighbours,
Elisabeth said.

He probably can't speak very good English, her
mother said. You can't just go bothering old frail
people.

He's not frail, Elisabeth said. He's not foreign.
He's not old. He doesn't look in the least
imprisoned.

He doesn't look what? her mother said.

It has to be done for tomorrow, Elisabeth said.

I've an idea, her mother said. Why don't you
make it up? Pretend you're asking him the
questions. Write down the answers you think
he'd give.

It's supposed to be true, Elisabeth said. It's for News.

They'll never know, her mother said. Make it up. The real news is always made up anyway.

The real news is *not* made up, Elisabeth said. It's the *news*.

That's a discussion we'll have again when you're a bit older, her mother said. Anyway. It's much harder to make things up. I mean, to make them up really well, well enough so that they're convincing. It requires much more skill. Tell you what. If you make it up and it's convincing enough to persuade Miss Simmonds that it's true, I'll buy you that Beauty and the Beast thing.

The video? Elisabeth said. Really?

Uh huh, her mother said, pivoting on one foot to look at herself from the side.

In any case our video player is broken, Elisabeth said.

If you persuade her, her mother said. I'll splash out on a new one.

Do you mean it? Elisabeth said.

And if Miss Simmonds gives you a hard time because it's made up, I'll ring the school and assure her that it's not made up, it's true, her mother said. Okay?

Elisabeth sat down at the computer desk.

If he *was* very old, the neighbour, he didn't look anything like the people who were meant to be it on

TV, who always seemed as if they were trapped inside a rubber mask, not just a face-sized mask, but one that went the length of the body from head to foot, and if you could tear it off or split it open it was like you'd find an untouched unchanged young person inside, who'd simply step cleanly out of the old fake skin, like the skin after you take out the inner banana. When they were trapped inside that skin, though, the eyes of people, at least the people in all the films and comedy programmes, looked desperate, like they were trying to signal to outsiders without giving the game away that they'd been captured by empty aged selves which were now keeping them alive inside them for some sinister reason, like those wasps that lay eggs inside other creatures so their hatchlings will have something to eat. Except the other way round, the old self feeding off the young one. All that was left would be the eyes, pleading, trapped behind the eyeholes.

Her mother was at the front door.

Bye, she called. Back soon.

Elisabeth ran through to the hall.

If I want to write the word elegant how do I spell it?

The front door closed.

Next evening after supper her mother folded the Newsbook jotter open at the page and went out the back door and down the garden to the still-sunny back fence, where she leaned over and waved the jotter in the air.

Hi, she said.

Elisabeth watched from the back door. The neighbour was reading a book and drinking a glass of wine in what was left of the sun. He put his book down on the garden table.

Oh hello, he said.

I'm Wendy Demand, she said. I'm your next door neighbour. I've been meaning to come and say hi since my daughter and I moved in.

Daniel Gluck, he said from the chair.

Lovely to meet you, Mr Gluck, her mother said.

Daniel, please, he said.

He had a voice off old films where things happen to well-dressed warplane pilots in black and white.

And, well, I really don't want to bother you, her mother said. But it suddenly struck me, and I hope you don't mind, and you don't think it's cheeky. I thought you might like to read this little piece that my daughter wrote about you for a school exercise.

About me? the neighbour said.

It's lovely, her mother said. A Portrait In Words Of Our Next Door Neighbour. Not that I come out of it very well myself. But I read it and then I saw you were out in the garden, and I thought, well. I mean it's charming. I mean it puts me to shame. But it's very fetching about you.

Elisabeth was appalled. She was appalled from head to foot. It was like the notion of appalled had

48

opened its mouth and swallowed her whole, exactly like an old-age rubberized skin would.

She stepped back behind the door where she couldn't be seen. She heard the neighbour scraping his chair on the flagstone. She heard him coming over to her mother at the fence.

When she came home from school next day the neighbour was sitting crosslegged on his garden wall right next to the front gate she needed to go through to get into the house.

She stopped stock still at the corner of the road.

She would walk past and pretend she didn't live in the house they lived in.

He wouldn't recognize her. She would be a child from another street altogether.

She crossed the road as if she were walking past. He unfolded his legs and he stood up.

When he spoke, there was nobody else in the road, so it was definitely to her. There was no getting out of it.

Hello, he said from his own side of the road. I was hoping I might run into you. I'm your neighbour. I'm Daniel Gluck.

I am not actually Elisabeth Demand, she said.

She kept walking.

Ah, he said. You're not. I see.

I am someone else, she said.

She stopped on the other side of the street and turned.

It was my sister who wrote it, she said.

I see, he said. Well, I had something I wanted to tell you, regardless.

What? Elisabeth said.

It's that I think your surname is originally French, Mr Gluck said. I think it comes from the French words de and monde, put together, which means, when you translate it, of the world.

Really? Elisabeth said. We always thought it meant like the asking kind of demand.

Mr Gluck sat down on the kerb and wrapped his arms round his knees. He nodded.

Of the world, or in the world, I think so, yes, he said. It might also mean of the people. Like Abraham Lincoln said. Of the people, by the people, for the people.

(He wasn't old. She was right. Nobody truly old sat with their legs crossed or hugged their knees like that. Old people couldn't do anything except sit in front rooms as if they'd been stunned by stun guns.)

I know that my – my sister's – Christian name, I mean the name Elisabeth, is meant to mean something about making promises to God, Elisabeth said. Which is a little difficult, because I'm not completely sure I believe in one, I mean, *she* does. I mean, doesn't.

Something else we have in common, he said, she and I. In fact, according to the history I've

50

happened to live through, I'd say that her first name, Elisabeth, means that one day she'll probably, quite unexpectedly against the odds, find herself being made queen.

A queen? Elisabeth said. Like you?

Um –, the neighbour said.

I myself think it would be really good, Elisabeth said, because of all the arty art you get to have all round you all the time.

Ah, the neighbour said. Right.

But does the name Elisabeth still mean that thing even if it's spelt with an s not a z? Elisabeth said.

Oh yes, indubitably, he said.

Elisabeth crossed to the same side of the road as the neighbour. She stood a little distance away.

What does your name mean? she said.

It means I'm lucky and happy, he said. The Gluck part. And that if I'm ever thrown into a pit that's full of hungry lions I'll survive. That's the first name. And if you ever have a dream and you don't know what it means you can ask me. My first name also designates an ability to interpret dreams.

Can you? Elisabeth said.

She sat down on her own piece of kerb only slightly along from the neighbour.

Actually I'm extremely bad at it, he said. But I can make up something useful, entertaining, perspicacious and kind. We have this in common, you and I. As well as the capacity to become someone else, if we so choose.

You mean you have it in common with my sister, Elisabeth said.

I do, the neighbour said. Very pleased to meet you both. Finally.

How do you mean, finally? Elisabeth said. We only moved here six weeks ago.

The lifelong friends, he said. We sometimes wait a lifetime for them.

He held his hand out. She got up, crossed the distance and held her own hand out. He shook her hand.

See you later, unexpected queen of the world. Not forgetting the people, he said.

It is just over a week since the vote. The bunting in the village where Elisabeth's mother now lives is up across the High Street for its summer festival, plastic reds and whites and blues against a sky that's all threats, and though it's not actually raining right now and the pavements are dry, the wind rattling the plastic triangles against themselves means it sounds all along the High Street like rain is hammering down.

The village is in a sullen state. Elisabeth passes a cottage not far from the bus stop whose front, from the door to across above the window, has been painted over with black paint and the words GO and HOME.

People either look down, look away or stare her out. People in the shops, when she buys some fruit, some ibuprofen and a newspaper for her mother, speak with a new kind of detachment. People she passes on the streets on the way from the bus stop to her mother's house regard her, and each other, with a new kind of loftiness.

Her mother, who tells her when she gets there that half the village isn't speaking to the other half of the village, and that this makes almost no difference to her since no one in the village speaks to her anyway or ever has though she's lived here nearly a decade now (in this her mother is being a touch melodramatic), is doing some hammering herself, nailing to the kitchen wall an old Ordnance Survey map of where she now lives, which she bought yesterday in a shop that used to be the local electrician's business and electrical appliances store and is now a place selling plastic starfish, pottery looking things, artisan gardening tools and canvas gardening gloves that look like they've been modelled on a 1950s utilitarian utopia.

The kind of shop with the kinds of things that look nice, cost more than they should and persuade you that if you buy them you'll be living the right kind of life, her mother says between lips still holding two little nails.

The map is from 1962. Her mother has drawn a red line with a Sharpie all round the coast marking where the new coast is.

She points to a spot quite far inland, on the new red line.

That's where the World War II pillbox fell into the sea ten days ago, she says.

She points to the other side of the map, furthest from the coast.

That's where the new fence has gone up, she says. Look.

She is pointing to the word *common* in the phrase *common land*.

Apparently a fence three metres high with a roll of razorwire along the top of it has been erected across a stretch of land not far from the village. It has security cameras on posts all along it. It encloses a piece of land that's got nothing in it but furze, sandy flats, tufts of long grass, scrappy trees, little clumps of wildflower.

Go and see it, her mother says. I want you to do something about it.

What can I do about it? Elisabeth says. I'm a lecturer in history of art.

Her mother shakes her head.

You'll know what to do, she says. You're young. Come on. We'll both go.

They walk along the single-track road. The grass is high on either side of them.

Can't believe he's still alive, your Mr Gluck, her mother is saying.

That's what everybody in The Maltings Care Providers plc pretty much says too, Elisabeth says.

He was so old back *then*, her mother says. He

must be more than a hundred. He must be. He was eighty back in the 90s. He used to walk up the street, remember, all bowed with age.

I don't remember that at all, Elisabeth says.

Like he carried the weight of the world on his back, her mother says.

You always said he was like a dancer, Elisabeth says.

An old dancer, her mother says. He was all bent over.

You used to say he was lithe, Elisabeth says.

Then she says,

oh dear God.

In front of them, slicing straight across a path Elisabeth's walked several times since her mother came to live here, and blocking the way as far as the eye can see no matter which way she turns her head, is a mass of chainlink metal.

Her mother sits down on the churned-up ground near the fence.

I'm tired, she says.

It's only two miles, Elisabeth says.

That's not what I mean, she says. I'm tired of the news. I'm tired of the way it makes things spectacular that aren't, and deals so simplistically with what's truly appalling. I'm tired of the vitriol. I'm tired of the anger. I'm tired of the meanness. I'm tired of the selfishness. I'm tired of how we're doing nothing to stop it. I'm tired of how we're encouraging it. I'm tired of the violence there is and I'm tired of the violence that's on its way, that's coming, that hasn't happened yet. I'm tired of liars. I'm tired of sanctified liars. I'm tired of how those liars have let this happen. I'm tired of having to wonder whether they did it out of stupidity or did it on purpose. I'm tired of lying governments. I'm tired of people not caring whether they're being lied to any more. I'm tired of being made to feel this fearful. I'm tired of animosity. I'm tired of pusillanimosity.

I don't think that's actually a word, Elisabeth says.

I'm tired of not knowing the right words, her mother says.

Elisabeth thinks of the bricks of the old broken-up pillbox under the water, the air bubbles rising from their pores when the tide covers them.

I'm a brick under water, she thinks.

Her mother, sensing her daughter's attention wandering, sags momentarily towards the fence.

Elisabeth, who is tired of her mother (already, and she's only an hour and a half into the visit) points to the little clips placed at different positions along the wire.

Careful, she says. I think it's electrified.

All across the country, there was misery and rejoicing. All across the country, what had happened whipped about by itself as if a live electric wire had snapped off a pylon in a storm and was whipping about in the air above the trees, the roofs, the traffic.

All across the country, people felt it was the wrong thing. All across the country, people felt it was the right thing. All across the country, people felt they'd really lost. All across the country, people felt they'd really won. All across the country, people felt they'd done the right thing and other people had done the wrong thing. All across the country, people looked up Google: *what is EU?* All across the country, people looked up Google: *move to Scotland.* All across the country, people looked up Google: *Irish passport applications.* All across the country, people called each other cunts. All across the country, people felt unsafe. All across the country, people were laughing their heads off. All across the country, people felt legitimized. All across the country, people felt bereaved and shocked. All across the country, people felt righteous. All across the country, people felt sick. All across the country, people felt history at their shoulder. All across the country, people felt history meant nothing. All across the country, people felt like they counted for nothing. All across the country, people had pinned their hopes on it. All across the country, people waved flags in the rain. All across the country, people drew swastika graffiti. All across the country, people threatened other people. All across the country, people told people to leave. All across the country, the media was insane. All across the country, politicians lied. All across the country, politicians fell apart. All across the country, politicians vanished. All across the country, promises vanished. All across the country, money vanished. All across the country, social media did the job. All across the country, things got nasty. All across the country, nobody spoke about it. All across the country, nobody spoke about anything else. All across the country, racist bile was general. All across the country, people said it wasn't that they didn't like immigrants. All across the country, people said it was about control. All across the country, everything changed overnight. All across the country, the haves and the have nots stayed the same. All across the country, the usual tiny per cent of the people made their money out of the usual huge per cent of the people. All across the country, money money money money. All across the country, no money no money no money no money.

All across the country, the country split in pieces. All across the country, the countries cut adrift.

All across the country, the country was divided, a fence here, a wall there, a line drawn here, a line crossed there,
a line you don't cross here,
a line you better not cross there,
a line of beauty here,
a line dance there,
a line you don't even know exists here,
a line you can't afford there,
a whole new line of fire,
line of battle,
end of the line,
here/there.

It was a typically warm Monday in late September 2015, in Nice, in the south of France. People out on the street were staring at the exterior of the Palais de la Préfccture where a long red banner with a swastika at the top of it had just coursed down the length of the front of the building and was settling itself against the balconies. Some people screamed. There was a flurry of shouting and pointing.

It was just a film production unit filming an adaptation of a memoir, using the Palais to recreate the Hôtel Excelsior, where Alois Brunner, the SS officer, had had his office and living quarters after the Italians surrendered to the Allies and the Gestapo had taken over in their place.

The Daily Telegraph reported next day on how the local authorities were apologizing for not having given enough notice about the film unit's plans to people who lived in the city, and how public confusion and offence had soon shifted to a mass taking of selfies.

It ran an online survey at the end of the news story. Were locals right to be angry about the banner: Yes or No?

Nearly four thousand people voted. Seventy per cent said no.

It was a typically warm Friday in late September 1943, in Nice, in the south of France. Hannah Gluck, who was twenty two years old (and whose real name wasn't on her identity papers, which stated that her name was Adrienne Albert), was sitting on the floor in the back of a truck. They'd picked up nine so far, all women, Hannah didn't know any of them. She and the woman opposite her exchanged looks. The woman looked down, then she looked back up, exchanged the look with Hannah one more time. Then they both lowered their eyes and looked down at the metal floor of the truck.

There were no accompanying vehicles. There were, in total, a driver plus a guard and a single quite young officer up front, and the two at the back, both even younger. The truck was part-open, part-roofed with canvas. The people on the streets could see their heads and the guards as they went past. Hannah had heard the officer saying to one of the men at the back as she climbed into the truck, keep it calm.

But the people on the street were oblivious, or made themselves it. They looked and looked away. They looked. But they weren't looking.

The streets were bright and splendid. The sun sent shockingly beautiful light off the buildings into the back of the truck.

When they stopped up a sidestreet to pick up two more, Hannah's eyes met again the eyes of the woman opposite. The woman moved her head with near-invisible assent.

The truck jolted to a stop. Traffic snarl-up. They'd taken the stupidest route. Good, and her sense of smell told her, the Friday fishmarket, busy.

Hannah stood up.

One of the guards told her to sit down.

The woman opposite stood up. One by one all the other women in the truck took their cue and stood up. The guard yelled at them to sit down. Both guards yelled. One waved a gun in the air at them.

This city isn't used to it yet, Hannah thought.

Get out of the way, the woman who'd nodded to Hannah said to the men. You can't kill us all.

Where are you taking them?

A woman had come over to the side of the truck and was looking in. A small gathering of women from the market, elegant women, headscarfed fish-seller girls and older women, formed behind her.

Then the officer got out of the truck and pushed the woman who'd asked where they were taking the women in the face. She fell and hit her head against a stone bollard. Her elegant hat fell off.

The women in that small gathering on the side of the road moved closer together. Their hush was audible. It spread back across the market like shadow, like cloud-cover.

It was a hush, Hannah thought, related to the quiet that comes over wildlife, happens to the birdsong, in an eclipse of the sun when something like night happens but it's the middle of the day.

Excuse me, ladies, Hannah said. This is where I get off.

The body of women on the truck huddled aside, let her through, let her go first.

**It was another Friday in the October holidays in
1995.** Elisabeth was eleven years old.

Mr Gluck from next door is going to look after
you today, her mother said. I have to go to London
again.

I don't need Daniel to look after me, Elisabeth
said.

You are eleven years old, her mother said. You
don't get a choice here. And don't call him Daniel.
Call him Mr Gluck. Be polite.

What would you know about politeness?
Elisabeth said.

Her mother gave her a hard look and said the
thing about her being like her father.

Good, Elisabeth said. Because I wouldn't want to
end up being anything like you.

Elisabeth locked the front door after her mother.

She locked the back door too. She drew the curtains in the front room and sat dropping lit matches on to the sofa to test how fireproof the new three piece suite really was.

She saw through a crack in the curtains Daniel coming up the front path. She opened the door even though she'd decided she wasn't going to.

Hello, he said. What you reading?

Elisabeth showed him her empty hands.

Does it look like I'm reading anything? she said.

Always be reading something, he said. Even when we're not physically reading. How else will we read the world? Think of it as a constant.

A constant what? Elisabeth said.

A constant constancy, Daniel said.

They went for a walk along the canal bank. Every time they passed someone, Daniel said hello. Sometimes the people said hello back. Sometimes they didn't.

It's really not all right to talk to strangers, Elisabeth said.

It is when you're as old as I am, Daniel said. It's not all right for a personage of your age.

I am tired of being a personage of my age and of having no choices, Elisabeth said.

Never mind that, Daniel said. That'll pass in the blink of an eye. Now. Tell me. What you reading?

The last book I read was called Jill's Gymkhana, Elisabeth said.

Ah. And what did it make you think about?
Daniel said.

Do you mean, what was it about? Elisabeth said.

If you like, Daniel said.

It was about a girl whose father has died,
Elisabeth told him.

Curious, Daniel said. It sounded like it might be
more about horses.

There's a lot of horse stuff *in* it, obviously,
Elisabeth said. In fact, the father who dies isn't
actually in it. He isn't in it at all. Except that him not
being there is the reason they move house, and her
mother has to work, and the daughter gets interested
in horses, and a gymkhana happens, and so on.

Your father's not dead, though? Daniel said.

No, Elisabeth said. He's in Leeds.

The word gymkhana, Daniel said, is a wonderful
word, a word grown from several languages.

Words don't get grown, Elisabeth said.

They do, Daniel said.

Words aren't plants, Elisabeth said.

Words are themselves organisms, Daniel said.

Oregano-isms, Elisabeth said.

Herbal and verbal, Daniel said. Language is like
poppies. It just takes something to churn the earth
round them up, and when it does up come the
sleeping words, bright red, fresh, blowing about.
Then the seedheads rattle, the seeds fall out. Then
there's even more language waiting to come up.

Can I ask you a question that's not about me or my life in any way or about my mother's life in any way either? Elisabeth said.

You can ask me anything you like, Daniel said. But I can't promise to answer what you ask unless I know a good enough answer.

Fair enough, Elisabeth said. Did you ever go to hotels with people and at the same time pretend to a child you were meant to be being responsible for that you were doing something else?

Ah, Daniel said. Before I answer that, I need to know whether there's an implicit moral judgement in your question.

If you don't want to answer the question I asked you, Mr Gluck, you should just say so, Elisabeth said.

Daniel laughed. Then he stopped laughing.

Well, it depends on what your question really is, he said. Is it about the act of going to the hotel? Or is it about the people who do or don't go to the hotel? Or is it about the pretending? Or is it about the act of pretending something to a child?

Yes, Elisabeth said.

In which case, is it a personal question to me, Daniel said, about whether I myself ever went to a hotel with someone? And in doing so chose to pretend to someone else that I wasn't doing what I was doing? Or is it about whether it matters that the person I may or may not have pretended to was a child rather than an adult? Or is it more general than that, and you want to know whether it's wrong to pretend anything to a child?

All of the above, Elisabeth said.

You are a very smart young person, Daniel said.

I am planning to go to college when I leave school, Elisabeth said. If I can afford it.

Oh, you don't want to go to college, Daniel said.

I do, Elisabeth said. My mother was the first in my family ever to go, and I will be the next.

You want to go to collage, Daniel said.

I want to go to college, Elisabeth said, to get an education and qualifications so I'll be able to get a good job and make good money.

Yes, but to study what? Daniel said.

I don't know yet, Elisabeth said.

Humanities? Law? Tourism? Zoology? Politics? History? Art? Maths? Philosophy? Music? Languages? Classics? Engineering? Architecture? Economics? Medicine? Psychology? Daniel said.

All of the above, Elisabeth said.

That's why you need to go to collage, Daniel said.

You're using the wrong word, Mr Gluck, Elisabeth said. The word you're using is for when you cut out pictures of things or coloured shapes and stick them on paper.

I disagree, Daniel said. Collage is an institute of education where all the rules can be thrown into the air, and size and space and time and foreground and background all become relative, and because of these skills everything you think you know gets made into something new and strange.

Are you still using avoidance tactics about the question about the hotel? Elisabeth said.

Truthfully? Daniel said. Yes. Which game would you rather play? I'll give you a choice of two. One. Every picture tells a story. Two. Every story tells a picture.

What does every story tells a picture mean? Elisabeth said.

Today it means that I'll describe a collage to you, Daniel said, and you can tell me what you think of it.

Without actually seeing it? Elisabeth said.

By seeing it in the imagination, as far as you're concerned, he said. And in the memory, as far as I'm concerned.

They sat down on a bench. A couple of kids were fishing off the rocks ahead of them. Their dog was standing on the rocks and shaking canal water off its coat. The boys squealed and laughed when the water fanned out into the air off the dog and hit them.

Picture or story? Daniel said. You choose.

Picture, she said.

Okay, Daniel said. Close your eyes. Are they closed?

Yes, Elisabeth said.

The background is rich dark blue, Daniel said. A blue much darker than sky. On top of the dark blue, in the middle of the picture, there's a shape made of pale paper that looks like a round full moon. On top of the moon, bigger than the moon, there's a cut-out black and white lady wearing a swimsuit, cut from a newspaper or fashion magazine. And next to her, as if she's leaning against it, there's a giant human hand. And the giant hand is holding inside it a tiny hand, a baby's hand. More truthfully, the baby's hand is also holding the big hand, holding it by its thumb. Below all this, there's a stylized picture of a woman's face, the same face repeated several times, but with a different coloured curl of real hair hanging over its nose each time –

Like at the hairdresser? Like colour samples? Elisabeth said.

You've got it, Daniel said.

She opened her eyes. Daniel's were shut. She shut her own eyes again.

And way off in the distance, in the blue at the bottom of the picture, there's a drawing of a ship with its sails up, but it's small, it's the smallest thing in the whole collage.

Okay, Elisabeth said.

Finally, there's some pink lacy stuff, by which I mean actual material, real lace, stuck on to the picture in a couple of places, up near the top, then further down towards the middle too. And that's it. That's all I can recall.

Elisabeth opened her eyes. She saw Daniel open his eyes a moment later.

Later that night, when she was home and falling asleep on the couch in front of the TV, Elisabeth would remember seeing his eyes open, and how it was like that moment when you just happen to see the streetlights come on and it feels like you're being given a gift, or a chance, or that you yourself've been singled out and chosen by the moment.

What do you think? Daniel said.

I like the idea of the blue and the pink together, Elisabeth said.

Pink lace. Deep blue pigment, Daniel said.

I like that you could maybe touch the pink, if it was made of lace, I mean, and it would feel different from the blue.

Oh, that's good, Daniel said. That's very good.

I like how the little hand is holding the big hand as much as the big hand is holding the little hand, Elisabeth said.

Today I myself particularly like the ship, Daniel said. The galleon with the sails up. If I'm remembering rightly. If it's even there.

Does that mean it's a real picture? Elisabeth said. Not one you made up?

It's real, Daniel said. Well, it was once. A friend

of mine did it. An artist. But I'm making it up from memory. How did it strike your imagination?

Like it would be if I was taking drugs, Elisabeth said.

Daniel stopped on the canal path.

You've never taken drugs, he said. Have you?

No, but if I did, and everything was in my head all at once, all sort of crowding in, it would be a bit like it, Elisabeth said.

Dear God. You'll tell your mother we've been taking drugs all afternoon, Daniel said.

Can we go and see it? Elisabeth said.

See what? Daniel said.

The collage? Elisabeth said.

Daniel shook his head.

I don't know where it is, he said. It might be long gone by now. Goodness knows where those pictures are now in the world.

Where did you see it in the first place? Elisabeth said.

I saw it in the early 1960s, Daniel said.

He said it as if a time could be a place.

I was there the day she made it, he said.

Who? Elisabeth said.

The Wimbledon Bardot, Daniel said.

Who's that? Elisabeth said.

Daniel looked at his watch.

Come on, art student, he said. Pupil of my eye. Time to go.

Time flies, Elisabeth said.

Well, yes. It can do, Daniel said. Literally. Watch this.

Elisabeth doesn't remember much of the above.

She does remember, though, the day they were walking along the canal bank when she was small and Daniel took his watch off his wrist and threw it into the water.

She remembers the thrill, the absolute not-doneness of it.

She remembers there were two boys down on the rocks and they turned their heads as the watch arced through the air over them and hit the canal, and she remembers knowing that it was a watch, Daniel's watch, not just any old stone or piece of litter, flying through the air, and knowing too that there was no way those boys could know this, that only she and Daniel knew the enormity of what he'd just done.

She remembers that Daniel had given her the choice, *to throw or not to throw.*

She remembers she chose *to throw.*

She remembers coming home with something amazing to tell her mother.

Here's something else from another time, from when Elisabeth was thirteen, that she also only remembers shreds and fragments of.

And anyway, why else are you always hanging round an old gay man?

(That was her mother.)

I don't *have* a father fixation, Elisabeth said. And Daniel's not gay. He's European.

Call him Mr Gluck, her mother said. And how do you know he's not gay? And if that's true, and he's not gay, then what does he want with you?

Or if he is, Elisabeth said, then he's not *just* gay. He's not *just* one thing or another. Nobody is. Not even you.

Her mother was ultra-sensitive and ultra-irritating right now. It was something to do with

Elisabeth being thirteen, not twelve. Whatever it was about, it was ultra-annoying.

Don't be rude, her mother said. And what you are is thirteen years old. You've got to be a bit careful of old men who want to hang around thirteen year old girls.

He's my friend, Elisabeth said.

He's eighty five, her mother said. How is an eighty five year old man your friend? Why can't you have normal friends like normal thirteen year olds?

It depends on how you'd define normal, Elisabeth said. Which would be different from how I'd define normal. Since we all live in relativity and mine at the moment is not and I suspect never will be the same as yours.

Where are you learning to talk like this? her mother said. Is that what you do on those walks?

We just walk, Elisabeth said. We just talk.

About what? her mother said.

Nothing, Elisabeth said.

About me? her mother said.

No! Elisabeth said.

What, then? her mother said.

About stuff, Elisabeth said.

What stuff? her mother said.

Stuff, Elisabeth said. He tells me about books and things.

Books, her mother said.

Books. Songs. Poets, Elisabeth said. He knows
about Keats. Season of mists. Opening an opiate.

He opened a what? her mother said.

He knows about Dylan, Elisabeth said.

Bob Dylan? her mother said.

No, the other Dylan, Elisabeth said. He knows it
off by heart, a lot of it. Though he did meet the
singer Bob Dylan once, when Bob Dylan was
staying with his friend.

He told you he's friends with Bob Dylan? her
mother said.

No. He met him. It was one winter. He was
sleeping on a friend's floor.

Bob Dylan? On a *floor*? her mother said. I don't
think so. Bob Dylan has always been a huge
international star.

And he knows about that poet you like who
killed herself, Elisabeth said.

Plath? her mother said. About suicide?

You so don't get it, Elisabeth said.

What exactly don't I get about an old man
putting ideas about suicide and a lot of lies about
Bob Dylan into my thirteen year old daughter's
head? her mother said.

And anyway, Daniel says it doesn't matter how
she died so long as you can still say or read her
words. Like the line about no longer grieving, and
the one about daughters of the darkness still
flaming like Guy Fawkes, Elisabeth said.

That doesn't sound like Plath, her mother said.

No, I'm almost completely sure I've never come across that line in any Plath I've read, and I've read it all.

It's Dylan. And the line about how love is evergreen, Elisabeth said.

What else does Mr Gluck tell you about love? her mother said.

He doesn't. He tells me about paintings, Elisabeth said. Pictures.

He shows you pictures? her mother said.

By a tennis player he knew, Elisabeth said. They're pictures people can't actually go and see. So he tells me them.

Why can't people see them? her mother said.

They just can't, Elisabeth said.

Private pictures? her mother said.

No, Elisabeth said. They're, like. Ones he knows.

Of tennis players? her mother said. Tennis players doing what?

No, Elisabeth said.

Oh God, her mother said. What have I done?

What you've done is used Daniel as my unofficial babysitter for years, Elisabeth said.

I told you. Call him *Mr Gluck*, her mother said. And I haven't been using him. That's just not true. And I want to know. I want to know in detail. Pictures of what?

Elisabeth made an exasperated sound.

I don't know, she said. People. Things.

What are the people doing in these pictures? her
mother said.

Elisabeth sighed. She shut her eyes.

Open your eyes right now Elisabeth, her
mother said.

I have to close my eyes or I can't see them,
Elisabeth said. Okay? Right. Marilyn Monroe
surrounded by roses, and then bright pink and
green and grey waves painted all round her. Except
that the picture isn't literally of literal Marilyn, it's
a picture of a picture of her. That's important to
remember.

Oh is it? her mother said.

Like if I was to take a photo of you and then
paint a picture of the photo, not you. And the roses
look a bit like flowery wallpaper rather than roses.
But the roses have also come out of the wallpaper
and have curled up round her collarbone, like
they're embracing her.

Embracing, her mother said. I see.

And someone French, someone famous in France
once, a man, he's wearing a hat and sunglasses, and
the top of the hat is a pile of red petals like a huge
red flower, and he's grey and black and white like a
picture in a paper, and behind him is all bright
orange, partly like a cornfield or golden grass, and
above him is a row of hearts.

Her mother had her hands over her own eyes at
the kitchen table.

Keep going, she said.

Elisabeth shut her eyes again.

One with a woman, not a famous person, she's just any woman and she's laughing, she's sort of throwing her arms up in a blue sky, and behind her at the foot of the picture there are alps, but very small, and a lot of zigzags in colours. And instead of having a body or clothes, the woman's insides are made up of pictures, pictures of other things.

He told you about a woman's body, a woman's insides, her mother said.

No, Elisabeth said. He told me about a woman whose body is made up of pictures instead of body. It's perfectly clear.

What pictures? Pictures of what? her mother said.

Things. Things that happen in the world, Elisabeth said. A sunflower. A man with a machine gun like out of a gangster film. A factory. A Russian looking politician. An owl, an exploding airship –

And Mr Gluck makes these pictures up in his head and puts them inside a woman's body? her mother said.

No, they're real, Elisabeth said. There's one called It's a Man's World. It's got a stately home in it, and the Beatles and Elvis Presley and a president in the back of a car getting shot.

That was when her mother started really yelling.

So she decided not to tell her mother about the collages with the children's heads being snipped off with the giant secateurs, and the massive hand coming out of the roof of the Albert Hall.

She decided not to mention the painting of a woman sitting on a backwards-turned chair with no clothes on, who brought a government down, and all the red paint and the black smudges through the red, that look, Daniel says, like *nuclear fallout*.

Even so, her mother still said it at the end of their talk

(and this is what Elisabeth does remember, verbatim, nearly two decades later, of the above conversation):

Unnatural.

Unhealthy.

You're not to.

I forbid it.

That's enough.

A minute ago it was June. Now the weather is September. The crops are high, about to be cut, bright, golden.

November? unimaginable. Just a month away.

The days are still warm, the air in the shadows sharper. The nights are sooner, chillier, the light a little less each time.

Dark at half past seven. Dark at quarter past seven, dark at seven.

The greens of the trees have been duller since August, since July really.

But the flowers are still coming. The hedgerows are still humming. The shed is already full of apples and the tree's still covered in them.

The birds are on the powerlines.

The swifts left weeks ago. They're hundreds of miles from here by now, somewhere over the ocean.

2

But now? The old man (Daniel) opens his eyes to find he can't open his eyes.

He seems to be shut inside something remarkably like the trunk of a Scots pine.

At least, it smells like a pine.

He's got no real way of telling. He can't move. There's not much room for movement inside a tree. His mouth and eyes are resined shut.

There are worse tastes to have in a mouth though, truth be told, and the trunks of Scots pines do tend to be narrow. Straight and tall, because this is the kind of tree good for telegraph poles, for the props that pit builders used in the days when industry relied on people working in pits and pits relied on pitprops to hold the ceilings of the tunnels up safely over their heads.

If you have no choice but to go underground, go in the form of something useful. If you have to be cut down, good to spend the afterlife as messenger between people across landscapes. Pines are tall. It's a lot better than being confined in a dwarf conifer.

From the top of a Scots pine it's possible to see quite a distance.

Daniel in the bed, inside the tree, isn't panicking. He isn't even claustrophobic. It's reasonable in here, excepting the paralysis, and perhaps it won't last. Let's be hopeful. No, in actual fact he's pleased to be being held immobile inside not just any old tree but such an ancient and adaptable and noble species, the kind of tree that pre-dates by quite a long way the sorts of trees with leaves; a versatile tree, the Scots pine doesn't need much soil depth, is remarkably good at long life, a tree that can last for many centuries. But the best thing of all about being inside this of all trees is the fact that it's more versatile, when it comes to colour, than your average general tree. The green of a forest of Scots pines can verge towards blue. And then in the spring there's the pollen, as yellow as bright paint pigment in an artist's jar, plentiful, pervasive, scene-stealing like the smoke round a conjuring trick. Back in the old days, the primeval days, the people who wanted others to think they had special powers used to fling such pollen about in the air around them. They would come to the woods and collect it to take home and use it as part of their act.

One might imagine it'd be unpleasant, being sealed inside a tree. One might imagine, ah, pining. But the scent lightens despair. It's perhaps a little like wearing a coat of armour except much nicer, because the armour is made of a substance through which the years themselves, formative, have run.

Oh.

A girl.

Who's she?

She vaguely resembles all the pictures in the papers, back then, of,

what's her name,

Keeler. Christine.

Yes. It's her.

Probably nobody knows who she is any more. Probably what was history then is nothing but footnote now, and on that note, he notes she's barefoot, alone in the summer night light of the hall of the great stately house where, by coincidence (history, footnote), he happens to know that the song Rule Britannia was first ever sung. She is standing next to a tapestried wall and she is slipping out of her summer dress.

It falls to the floor. Up go all his pinecones. He groans. She doesn't hear a thing.

She unhooks the armour off its stand and sorts it

into pieces on the parquet floor. She fits the breastplate over her (quite magnificent, it's all true) chest. She puts her arms through the armholes. There's no metal cover at all at the place where her, ah, lower underwear is. She puts her hands down to the space in the metal there as if she's just realized how she's likely to reveal herself, through this gap, when fully armoured.

She wriggles herself out of what's left of her underwear.

It falls to the floor.

He groans.

She steps out of it, leaves it on the carpet runner. It lies there. It looks like a boned blackbird.

She fits one leg-piece to a thigh, then the next. She yelps and swears – sharp edge maybe, inside the second of the leg-pieces? She straps the leg-pieces to the backs of her thighs and slips a bare foot inside the first huge boot. She slips her arms inside the metal arm-pieces, lifts the helmet and fits it over her hair. Through the slits in its front she looks around for the gauntlets. One on. Now the next.

She pushes up the visor with her metal hand and her eyes look out.

She goes and stands in front of a huge old mirror hung on the wall. Her laugh comes tinnily out through the helmet. She knocks the visor down again with the gauntlet edge. The only thing visible of her is her privates.

Then she sets off, but delicately, so anything loosely strapped won't fall off. She clinks her way down the corridor quite as if a suit of armour isn't nearly as heavy as it looks.

When she comes to a door she turns and pushes it. It opens. She disappears.

The room she's just entered explodes into raucous laughter.

Can laughter be well-heeled?

Is powerful laughter different from ordinary laughter?

That type of laughter is always powerful.

There's a song in this, Daniel thinks.

Ballad of Christine Keeler.

Well-heel-er. Dealer. Feeler. Squealer. Conceal her. Steal her. Mrs Peel her.

Ah, no. The fictional creation Mrs Peel came later, a couple of years after this creation.

But probably the Peel of Mrs is based, partly at least, on the Keel of Keeler, a suggestive little gift to the ear of the beholder.

Right now he's pressed so close between all the people up in the public gallery that – where now?

A courtroom.

The Old Bailey.

That summer.

He only imagined Keeler trying on the armour. He dreamed it, though it's rumoured to have happened.

But this, this below, about to happen, he witnessed.

First up, Keeler versus Ward, her friend, Stephen the osteopath, the portraitist. No suit of armour but nonetheless she's armoured here, sheet-metal listless. Impervious. Masked. Perfectly made-up. Dead with a hint of exotic.

She puts the place into a trance by speaking like someone in a trance might speak. Clever. Empty. Sexy automaton. Living doll. Sensational, the public gallery turns pubic gallery. No one can think of anything else, except her friend Stephen, down at the front, who every day picks up his pencil and sketches what he's seeing.

Meanwhile, days pass.

Down in the witness box, someone else now, a woman, a different one, a Miss Ricardo, truth be told she's even lower-class than poor Keeler, young, coiffed, roughed at the edges, her hair piled red and high on her head, a dancer, *I earn money by visiting men and being paid by them.*

She has just announced to the courtroom that the statements that she first made to the police about this case were untrue.

The crowd in the gallery presses forward even harder. Scandal and lies. What prostitutes do. But Daniel sees the woman, just a girl really, fighting to hold herself straight. He sees how her face, her whole demeanour, have gone something like pale green with the fear.

Red hair.

Green girl.

I didn't want my young sister to go to a remand home, the girl says. My baby taken away from me. The chief inspector told me they would take my sister and my baby if I didn't make the statements. He also threatened to have my brother nicked. I believed him and so I made the statements. But I have decided I don't want to give false evidence at the Old Bailey. I told The People newspaper. I want everyone to know why I lied.

Oh dear God.

She's green all right.

The prosecuting lawyer has an air of foxhound. He makes fun of her. He asks her why on earth she'd sign a statement in the first place if the statement she was signing wasn't true.

She tells him she wanted the police to leave her alone.

The prosecuting lawyer worries at her. Why has she never complained about any of this before now?

Who could I complain to? she says.

A deliberate liar, then, is she?

Yes, she says.

Daniel in the gallery sees one of her hands, the one on the rail of the witness box, cover itself in little shoots and buds. The buds split open. There are leaves coming out of her fingers.

The Judge advises her to take the time overnight very carefully to consider the version of things she's choosing to tell to the court today.

Blink of an eye.

Next day.

The girl's in the box again. Today she is almost all young tree. Now only her face and her hair are unleafy. Overnight, like a girl in a myth being hunted by a god who's determined to have his way with her, she has altered herself, remade herself so she can't be had by anyone.

The same men shout at her again. They're angry with her for not lying about lying. The prosecutor asks her why she told her story about lying to a newspaper reporter, not to the police. He suggests this was improper, an improper thing to do, the sort of thing an improper woman like this woman *would* do.

What would be the point, she says, in me going to tell the truth to the very people who've told me to lie?

The Judge sighs. He turns to the jury.

Dismiss this evidence from your minds, he says. I instruct you to disregard it altogether.

There's a song in this too, Daniel thinks as he watches the white bark rise up and cover her mouth, her nose, her eyes.

Ballad of the Silver Birch.

High church. Lurch. Besmirch. Soul search.

Himself, he goes straight from that courtroom to the house of the girl he's in love with.

(He's in love with her. He can hardly say her name to himself. He's in love with her so much.

She isn't in love with him. Only a few weeks back she married someone else. He can say her husband's name all right. His name's Clive.

But he's just seen a miraculous thing, hasn't he?

He's seen something that changes the nature of things.)

He stands in the rain in the back yard. It's dark now. He is looking up at the windows of the house. His hands and forearms, his face, his good shirt and suit are smeared from the dustbins and climbing the fence, as if he's still young enough to.

There is a famous short story, The Dead, by James Joyce, in which a young man stands at the back of a house and sings a song on a freezing night to a woman he loves. Then this young man, pining for the woman, dies. He catches a chill in the snow, he dies young. Height of romanticism! That woman in that story, for the rest of her life, has that young man's song always riddling through her like woodworm.

Well, Daniel himself's not a young man. That's partly the problem. The woman he's pretty much sure he loves more than anyone he's ever, the

woman he will pine away to nothing without the
love of, is twenty years younger than him, and,
yes, not that long ago, there *is* that, married
Clive.

And then there's the extra other matter, the
matter of not being able to sing. Well, not in tune.

But he can shout a song. He can shout the words.
And they're *his* words, not just any old words.

And she only knew him for ten days before she
married him, Clive, that is. There's always hope,
with this particular girl.

The Ballad of the Girl Who Keeps Telling
Me No.

Fast little number, witty, to meet her wit.

Throaty. Gloaty. Wild oat(y). Grace-note(y).
Misquote(y). Anecdote(y). Casting vote(y).
Furcoat(y). Petticoat(y). Torpedo boat(y).

(Terrible.)

I'm billy goaty.

Don't be haughty.

But no light comes on in any of the windows. It
takes about half an hour of standing in the rain for
him to admit there's nobody in, that he's been
standing in a yard shouting bad rhymes at a house
where nobody's home.

That fashionable swing-seat they've got in there
hanging from the ceiling in the living room will be
slowly turning this way and that by itself in
the dark.

Ironic. He's a sap. She'll never even know he was here, will she?

(True enough. She never knew.

And then what happened next, well, it happened next, and history, that other word for irony, went its own foul witty way, sang its own foul witty ditty, and the girl was the one who died young in this story.

Riddled. Woodworm. All through him.)

Then the old man confined in the bed in the tree, Daniel, is a boy on a train that's passing through deep spruce woods. He is thin and small, sixteen summers old but he thinks he's a man. It's summer again, he is on the continent, they are all on the continent, things are a little uneasy on the continent. Something's going to happen. It is already happening. Everybody knows. But everybody is pretending it's not happening.

All the people on the train can see from his clothes that he's not from here. But he can speak the language, though none of the strangers round him on the train knows he can, because they don't know who he is, or who she is, his sister next to him, they don't know the first thing about them.

The people round them are talking about the necessity of developing a scientific and legal means of gauging exactly who's what.

There is a professor at the institute, the man sitting across from him says to a woman. And this professor is engaged in inventing a modern tool to record, quite scientifically, certain physical statistics.

Oh? the woman says.

She nods.

Noses, ears, the spaces between, the man across from Daniel says.

He is flirting with that woman.

The measurement of parts of the body, most especially of the features of the head area, can tell you quite succinctly everything you need to know. Eye colour, hair colour, the sizing of foreheads. It's been done before, but never so expertly, never so exactly. It's a case in the first place of measuring and collating. But a slightly more complex case, in the long run, of the sifting of the collected statistics.

The boy smiles at his little sister.

She lives here all the time.

She is assiduously reading her book. He nudges her. She looks up from it. He winks.

She speaks it as her first language. She knows the flirting is the thinnest layer. She knows exactly what they're saying. She turns the page in her book, glances at him then at the people opposite over the top of it.

I hear them. But am I going to let it stop me reading?

She says this in English to her brother. She makes a face at him. Then she glances her whole self back down into the book.

Out in the train corridor, when the boy Daniel goes to relieve himself, there's a capped and booted man blocking the way. His front is all pockets and straps. His arms are stretched in a leisurely way from one side to the other of the passage through to the toilet and the other carriages. He is swaying with the movement of this train as it moves through the spruce woods and farmland almost as if he's a working part of its mechanical structure.

Can the sheer breadth of someone's chest be insidious?

Oh yes it can.

Lazy, sure, he smiles at the boy, the smile of a soldier in repose. He lifts one arm higher so the boy can pass under. As Daniel does, the soldier's arm comes down just far enough to brush, with the material of his shirt, the hair on the top of his head.

Hopla, the soldier says.

Boy on a train.

Blink of an eye.

Old man in a bed.

The old man in the bed is confined.

Wooden overcoat

(y).

Cut this tree I'm living in down. Hollow its trunk out.

Make me all over again, with what you scooped out of its insides.

Slide the new me back inside the old trunk.

Burn me. Burn the tree. Spread the ashes, for luck, where you want next year's crops to grow.
Birth me all over again
Burn me and the tree
Next summer's sun
Midwinter guarantee

It is still July. Elisabeth goes to her mother's medical practice in the middle of town. She waits in the queue of people. When she gets to the front she tells the receptionist that the GP her mother is registered with is at this practice, that she herself isn't registered with a GP here but that she's been feeling unwell so she'd like to talk to a doctor, probably not urgent, but something does feel wrong.

The receptionist looks Elisabeth's mother up on the computer. She tells Elisabeth that her mother isn't listed at this surgery.

Yes she is, Elisabeth says. She definitely is.

The receptionist clicks on another file and then goes to the back of the room and opens a drawer in a filing cabinet. She takes out a piece of paper, reads it, then puts it back in and shuts the drawer. She comes back and sits down.

She tells Elisabeth she's afraid that her mother is no longer listed on the patient list.

My mother definitely doesn't know that, Elisabeth says. She thinks she's a patient here. Why would you take her off the list?

The receptionist says that this is confidential information and that she's not permitted to tell Elisabeth anything about any patient other than Elisabeth herself.

Well, can I register and see someone anyway? Elisabeth says. I feel pretty rough. I'd really like to talk to someone.

The receptionist asks her if she has any ID.

Elisabeth shows the receptionist her library card for the university.

Valid until my job goes, at least, she says, now the universities are all going to lose 16 per cent of our funding.

The receptionist smiles a patient smile. (A smile especially for patients.)

I'm afraid we need something with a current address and preferably also with a photograph, she says.

Elisabeth shows her her passport.

This passport is expired, the receptionist says.

I know, Elisabeth says. I'm in the middle of renewing it.

I'm afraid we can't accept an expired ID, the receptionist says. Have you got a driving licence?

Elisabeth tells the receptionist she doesn't drive.
What about a utility bill? the receptionist says.
What, on me? Elisabeth says. Right now?

The receptionist says that it's a good idea always
to carry a utility bill around with you in case
someone needs to be able to verify your ID.

What about all the people who pay their bills
online and don't get paper bills any more?
Elisabeth says.

The receptionist looks longingly at a ringing
phone on the left of her desk. Still with her eyes on
the ringing phone she tells Elisabeth it's perfectly
easy to print a bill out on a standard inkjet.

Elisabeth says she's staying at her mother's, that
it's sixty miles away, and that her mother doesn't
have a printer.

The receptionist actually looks angry that
Elisabeth's mother might not have a printer. She
talks about catchment areas and registration of
patients. Elisabeth realizes she's suggesting that
now that her mother lives outside the catchment
area Elisabeth has no business being here in this
building.

It's also perfectly easy to mock up a bill and print
it out. To pretend to be a person, Elisabeth says.
And what about all the people doing scams? How
does having your name on a piece of printed-out
paper make you who you are?

She tells the receptionist about the scammer

calling him or her self Anna Pavlova, for whom NatWest bank statements have been regularly arriving for the past three years at her own flat, even though she's notified NatWest about it repeatedly and knows for sure no one called Anna Pavlova has lived there for at least a decade, having lived there herself that long.

So what does a piece of paper prove, exactly, in the end? Elisabeth says.

The receptionist looks at her and her face is stony. She asks if Elisabeth will excuse her for a moment. She answers the phone.

She gestures to Elisabeth to step back away from the desk while she takes this call. Then to make it even clearer she puts her hand over the receiver and says, if I could just ask you to let me accord this caller the requisite privacy.

There is a small queue of people forming behind Elisabeth all waiting to check in with this receptionist.

Elisabeth goes to the Post Office instead.

Today the Post Office is near empty, except for the queue waiting to use the self-service machines. Elisabeth takes a ticket. 39. Numbers 28 and 29 are apparently being served, though there's no one at the counter at all, on either the Post Office side or the customer side.

Ten minutes later a woman comes through the door at the back. She shouts the numbers 30 and 31.

No one responds. So she forwards the lit machine through the 30s, calling out the numbers as she does.

Elisabeth comes to the counter and gives the woman her passport envelope and the new photobooth shots, in which her face is definitely the right size (she has measured it). She shows her the receipt proving she paid the £9.75 Check & Send fee last week.

When are you planning to travel? the woman says.

Elisabeth shrugs. Nothing planned, she says.

The woman looks at the photographs.

There's a problem, I'm afraid, the woman says.

What? Elisabeth says.

This piece of hair here should be off the face, she says.

It *is* off the face, Elisabeth says. That's my forehead. It's not even touching the face.

It should be right back off the face, the woman says.

If I took a picture of myself with it not where it is, Elisabeth says, I wouldn't truly look like me. What would be the point of a passport photo that didn't actually look like me?

I'd say that's touching the eyes, the woman says.

The woman pushes her chair back and takes the photo sheet round to the counter where Travel Cash is issued. She shows it to a man there. The man comes back to the counter with her.

There may be a problem with your photograph,

he says, in that my colleague thinks the hair is touching the face in it.

In any case, the hair is irrelevant, the woman says. Your eyes are too small.

Oh God, Elisabeth says.

The man goes back to his Travel Cash counter. The woman is sliding the pictures of Elisabeth up and down inside a transparent plastic chart with markings and measurements in different boxes printed all over it.

Your eyes don't sit with the permissible regularity inside the shaded area, she says. This doesn't line up. This should be in the middle and, as you can see, it's at the side of your nose. I'm afraid these photographs don't meet the necessary stipulation. If you go to Snappy Snaps rather than to a booth –

That's exactly what the man I saw here last week said, Elisabeth says. What is it with this Post Office and its relationship with Snappy Snaps? Does someone's brother work at Snappy Snaps?

So you were advised to go to Snappy Snaps already but you chose not to go, the woman says.

Elisabeth laughs. She can't not; the woman looks so very stern about her not having gone to Snappy Snaps.

The woman lifts the chart and shows her again her own face with a shaded box over it.

I'm afraid it's a no, the woman says.

Look, Elisabeth says. Just send these photos to

the Passport Office. I'll take the risk. I think they'll be okay.

The woman looks wounded.

If they don't accept them, Elisabeth says, I'll come back in and see you again soon and tell you you were quite right and I was wrong, my hair was wrong and my eyes were in totally the wrong place.

No, because if you submit this through Check & Send today, this will be the last time this office will have anything to do with this application, the woman says. Once the application goes in, it's the Passport Office who'll be in touch with you about your unmet specifications.

Right, Elisabeth says. Thank you. Send them. I'll take my chances. And will you do me a favour?

The woman looks very alarmed.

Will you say hello to your colleague who works here who's got the seafood intolerance? Tell him the woman with the wrong size of head sends her best wishes and hopes he is well.

That description? the woman says. Forgive me, but. Could be anybody. One of thousands.

She writes in ballpoint on Elisabeth's receipt: *customer choosing to send photos at own risk.*

Elisabeth stands outside the Post Office. She feels better. It's cool, rainy.

She'll go and buy a book from that second-hand shop.

Then she'll go to see Daniel.

It takes a fragment of a fragment of a second for Elisabeth's data to go into the computer. Then the receptionist gives her back her scanned ID.

Daniel is asleep. A care assistant, a different one today, is swishing round the room with a mop that smells of pine cleaner.

Elisabeth wonders what's going to happen to all the care assistants. She realizes she hasn't so far encountered a single care assistant here who isn't from somewhere else in the world. That morning on the radio she'd heard a spokesperson say, *but it's not just that we've been rhetorically and practically encouraging the opposite of integration for _immigrants_ to this country. It's that we've been rhetorically and practically encouraging _ourselves_ not to integrate. We've been doing this as a matter of self-policing since Thatcher taught us to be*

selfish and not just to think but to believe that
there's no such thing as society.

Then the other spokesperson in the dialogue said,
well, you would say that. Get over it. Grow up.
Your time's over. Democracy. You lost.

It is like democracy is a bottle someone can
threaten to smash and do a bit of damage with. It
has become a time of people saying stuff to each
other and none of it actually ever becoming
dialogue.

It is the end of dialogue.

She tries to think when exactly it changed, how
long it's been like this without her noticing.

She sits down next to Daniel. Sleeping
Socrates.

How are you doing today, Mr Gluck? she says
quietly down by his sleeping ear.

She gets her new/old book out and opens it at its
beginning: *My purpose is to tell of bodies which*
have been transformed into shapes of a different
kind. You heavenly powers, since you were
responsible for those changes, as for all else, look
favourably on my attempts, and spin an unbroken
thread of verse, from the earliest beginnings of the
world, down to my own times.

Today Daniel looks like a child, but one with a
very old head.

As she watches him sleep she thinks about Anna
Pavlova, not the dancer, the scammer, who

registered a NatWest bank account at Elisabeth's address.

What kind of scammer names herself – assuming it's a her – after a ballet dancer? Did she really think people working at NatWest wouldn't question someone using the name Anna Pavlova? Or are accounts all set up by machine now and machines don't know how to quantify that stuff?

Then again, what does Elisabeth know? It's possible that it's not that unusual a name. Maybe there are a million and one Anna Pavlovas right now in the world. Maybe Pavlova is the Russian equivalent of Smith.

A cultured scammer. A sensitive scammer. A prima ballerina light on her feet brilliantly expressive prodigiously talented legendary scammer. A sleeping beauty dying swan kind of a scammer.

She remembers her mother believing at some point, way back in the beginning, that Daniel, because he was so thin, so Puck-like and lithe – so much so that even in his eighties he was better at getting up the ladder into their loft space than her mother, then in her forties, was – had once been a ballet dancer, was perhaps a famous dancer grown old.

Which would you choose? Daniel had said once. Should I please her and tell her she's guessed right, and that I'm a recently retired Rambert? Or should I tell her the more mundane truth?

113

Definitely tell her the lie, Elisabeth said.

But think what will happen if I do, Daniel said.

It'll be brilliant, Elisabeth said. It'll be really funny.

I'll tell you what will happen, Daniel said. This. You and I will know I've lied, but your mother won't. You and I will know something that your mother doesn't. That will make us feel different towards not just your mother, but each other. A wedge will come between us all. You will stop trusting me, and quite right, because I'd be a liar. We'll all be lessened by the lie. So. Do you still choose the ballet? Or will I tell the sorrier truth?

I want the lie, Elisabeth said. She knows loads of things I don't. I want to know some things she doesn't.

The power of the lie, Daniel said. Always seductive to the powerless. But how is my being a retired dancer going to help in any real way with your feelings of powerlessness?

Were you a dancer? Elisabeth said.

That's my secret, Daniel said. I'll never divulge. Not to any human being. Not for any money.

It was a Tuesday in March in 1998. Elisabeth was thirteen. She was out for a walk in the newly light early evening with Daniel, even though her mother had told her she wasn't to.

They walked past the shops, then over to the fields where the inter-school summer sports were held, where the fair went and the circus. Elisabeth had last come to the field just after the circus had left, especially to look at the flat dry place where the circus had had its tent. She liked doing melancholy things like that. But now you couldn't tell that any of these summer things had ever happened. There was just empty field. The sports tracks had faded and gone. The flattened grass, the places that had turned to mud where the crowds had wandered round between the rides and the open-sided trailers full of the driving and shooting games, the ghost circus ring: nothing but grass.

Somehow this wasn't the same as melancholy. It was something else, about how melancholy and nostalgia weren't relevant in the slightest. Things just happened. Then they were over. Time just passed. Partly it felt unpleasant, to think like that, rude even. Partly it felt good. It was kind of a relief.

Past the field there was another field. Then there was the river.

Isn't it a bit too far, to walk as far as the river? Elisabeth said.

She didn't want him to have to go so far if he really was as ancient as her mother kept saying.

Not for me, Daniel said. A mere bagatelle.

A what? Elisabeth said.

A trifle, Daniel said. Not *that* kind of trifle. A mere nothing. Something trifling.

What will we do all the way there and back? Elisabeth said.

We'll play Bagatelle, Daniel said.

Is Bagatelle really a game? Elisabeth said. Or did you just make it up right now on the spot?

I admit, it's a very new game to me too, Daniel said. Want to play?

Depends, Elisabeth said.

How we play is: I tell you the first line of a story, Daniel said.

Okay, Elisabeth said.

116

Then you tell me the story that comes into your head when you hear that first line, Daniel said.

Like, a story that already exists? Elisabeth said. Like Goldilocks and the three bears?

Those poor bears, Daniel said. That bad wicked rude vandal of a girl. Going into their house uninvited and unannounced. Breaking their furniture. Eating their supplies. Spraying her name with spraypaint on the walls of their bedrooms.

She does not spray her name on their walls, Elisabeth said. That's not in the story.

Who says? Daniel said.

The story is from really long ago, probably way before spraypaint existed, Elisabeth said.

Who says? Daniel said. Who says the story isn't happening right now?

I do, Elisabeth said.

Well, you're going to lose at Bagatelle, then, Daniel said, because the whole point of Bagatelle is that you trifle with the stories that people think are set in stone. And no, not *that* kind of trifle –

I know, Elisabeth said. Jeez. Don't demean me.

Demean you? Daniel said. Moi? Now. What kind of story do you want to trifle with? You can choose.

They'd come to a bench at the side of the river; both the fields were far behind them. It was the first time Elisabeth had ever crossed the fields without it seeming like it took a long time.

What's the available choice? Elisabeth said.

Can be anything, Daniel said.

Like truth or lies? That kind of choice?

A bit oppositional, but yes, if you choose, Daniel said.

Can I choose between war and peace? Elisabeth said.

(There was war on the news every day. There were sieges, pictures of bags that had bodies in them. Elisabeth had looked up in the dictionary the word massacre to check what it literally meant. It meant to kill a lot of people with especial violence and cruelty.)

Lucky for you, you've got some choice in the matter, Daniel said.

I choose war, Elisabeth said.

Sure you want war? Daniel said.

Is *sure you want war* the first line of the story? Elisabeth said.

It can be, Daniel said. If that's what you choose.

Who are the characters? Elisabeth said.

You make one up and I'll make one up, Daniel said.

A man with a gun, Elisabeth said.

Okay, Daniel said. And I choose a person who's come in disguise as a tree.

A what? Elisabeth said. No way. You're supposed to say something like another man with another gun.

Why am I? Daniel said.

Because it's war, Elisabeth said.

I have some input into this story too, and I choose a person who's wearing a tree costume, Daniel said.

Why? Elisabeth said.

Ingenuity, Daniel said.

Ingenuity won't win your character this game, Elisabeth said. My character's got a gun.

That's not all you've got and it's not your only responsibility here, Daniel said. You've also got a person with the ability to resemble a tree.

Bullets are faster and stronger than tree costumes and will rip through and obliterate tree costumes, Elisabeth said.

Is that the kind of world you're going to make up? Daniel said.

There is no point in making up a world, Elisabeth said, when there's already a real world. There's just the world, and there's the truth about the world.

You mean, there's the truth, and there's the made-up version of it that we get told about the world, Daniel said.

No. The *world* exists. *Stories* are made up, Elisabeth said.

But no less true for that, Daniel said.

That's ultra-crazy talk, Elisabeth said.

And whoever makes up the story makes up the world, Daniel said. So always try to welcome people into the home of your story. That's my suggestion.

How does making things up welcome people?
Elisabeth said.

What I'm suggesting, Daniel said, is, if you're
telling a story, always give your characters the same
benefit of the doubt you'd welcome when it comes
to yourself.

Like being on benefits? Like unemployment
benefit? Elisabeth said.

The necessary benefit of the doubt, Daniel said.
And always give them a choice – even those
characters like a person with nothing but a tree
costume between him or her and a man with a gun.
By which I mean characters who seem to have no
choice at all. Always give them a home.

Why should I? Elisabeth said. You didn't give
Goldilocks a home.

Did I stop her for one moment from going into
that house with her spraypaint can? Daniel said.

That's because you couldn't, Elisabeth said,
because it was already a part of the story that that's
what she does every time the story's told – she goes
into the bears' house. She has to. Otherwise there's
no story. Is there? Except the part with the
spraypaint can. The bit just made up by you.

Is my spraypaint can any more made up than the
rest of the story? Daniel said.

Yes, Elisabeth said.

Then she thought about it.

Oh! she said. I mean, no.

And if I'm the storyteller I can tell it any way I like, Daniel said. So, it follows. If *you* are –

So how do we ever know what's true? Elisabeth said.

Now you're talking, Daniel said.

And what if, right, Elisabeth said, what if Goldilocks was doing what she was doing because she had no choice? What if she was like seriously upset that the porridge was too hot, and that's what made her go ultra-crazy with the spraypaint can? What if cold porridge always made her feel really upset about something in her past? What if something that had happened in her life had been really terrible and the porridge reminded her of it, and that's why she was so upset that she broke the chair and unmade all the beds?

Or what if she was just a vandal? Daniel said, who went into places and defaced them for no reason other than that's what I, the person in charge of the story, have decided that all Goldilockses are like?

I personally shall be giving her the benefits of the doubt, Elisabeth said.

Now you're ready, Daniel said.

Ready for what? Elisabeth said.

Ready to bagatelle it as it is, Daniel said.

Time-lapse of a million billion flowers opening their heads, of a million billion flowers bowing, closing their heads again, of a million billion new flowers opening instead, of a million billion buds becoming leaves then the leaves falling off and rotting into earth, of a million billion twigs splitting into a million billion brand new buds.

Elisabeth, sitting in Daniel's room in The Maltings Care Providers plc just short of twenty years later, doesn't remember anything of that day or that walk or the dialogue described in that last section. But here, preserved, is the story Daniel actually told, rescued whole from the place in human brain cell storage which keeps intact but filed away the dimensionality of everything we ever experience (including the milder air that March evening, the smell of the new season in the air, the traffic noise in the distance and everything else her senses and her cognition comprehended of the time, the place, her presence in both).

There's no way I can be bothered to think up a story with the tree costume thing in it, Elisabeth said. Because nobody in their right minds could make that story any good.

Is this a challenge to my right mind? Daniel said.

Indubitably, Elisabeth said.

Well then, Daniel said. My right mind will meet your challenge.

Sure you want war? the person dressed as a tree said.

The person dressed as a tree was standing with its branches up in the air like someone with his or her hands up. A man with a gun was pointing the gun at the person dressed as a tree.

Are you threatening me? the man with the gun said.

No, the person dressed as a tree said. You're the one with the gun.

I'm a peaceable person, the man with the gun said. I don't want trouble. That's why I carry this gun. And it's not like I have anything against people like you generally.

What do you mean, people like me? the person dressed as a tree said.

What I said. People dressed in stupid pantomime tree costumes, the man with the gun said.

But why? the person dressed as a tree said.

Think what it'd be like if everyone started wearing tree costumes, the man with the gun said. It'd be like living in a wood. And we don't live in a wood. This town's been a town since long before I was born. If it was good enough for my parents, and my grandparents and my great grandparents.

What about your own costume? the person dressed as a tree said.

(The man with the gun was wearing jeans, a T-shirt and a baseball cap.)

This isn't a costume, the man said. These are my clothes.

Well, these are *my* clothes. But I'm not calling your clothes stupid, the person dressed as a tree said.

Yeah, because you wouldn't dare, the man with the gun said.

He waved his gun.

And anyway, yours *are* stupid clothes, he said. Normal people don't go around wearing tree costumes. At least, they don't round here. God knows what they do in other cities and towns, well, that's up to them. But if you got your way you'd be dressing our kids up as trees, dressing our women up as trees. It's got to be nipped in the bud.

The man with the gun raised it and pointed it. The person dressed as a tree braced him or her self inside the thick cotton. The little grassblades painted round the bottom of the costume shivered round the painted roots. The man looked down the sights of his gun. Then he lowered the gun away from his eyes. He laughed.

See, the funny thing is, he said, it just came into my head that in war films, when they're going to execute someone, they stand them up against trees or posts. So shooting you is a bit like not shooting anyone at all.

He put the gun to his eye. He aimed at the trunk of the tree, at roughly where he guessed the heart of the person inside the costume was.

So. That's me done, Daniel said.

You can't stop there! Elisabeth said. Mr Gluck!

Can't I? Daniel said.

Elisabeth sits in the anodyne room next to Daniel, holding the book open, reading about metamorphoses. Round them, invisible, splayed out across the universe, are all the shot-dead pantomime characters. The Dame is dead. The Ugly Sisters are dead. Cinderella and the Fairy Godmother and Aladdin and the cat with the boots and Dick Whittington, mown down, a panto corncrop, panto massacre, a comedy tragedy, dead, dead, dead.

Only the person dressed as a tree is still standing.

But just as the man with the gun is finally about to shoot, the person dressed as a tree transforms before the gunman's eyes into a real tree, a giant tree, a magnificent golden ash tree towering high above waving its mesmerizing leaves.

No matter how hard the man with the gun shoots at this tree he can't kill it with bullets.

So he kicks its thick trunk. He decides he'll go and buy weedkiller to pour on its roots, or matches and petrol, to burn it down. He turns to go – and that's when he gets kicked in the head by the half of the pantomime horse it's slipped his mind to shoot.

He falls to the ground, dead himself on top of the pantomime fallen. It's a surrealist vision of hell.

What's surrealist, Mr Gluck?

This is. There they lie. The rain falls. The wind blows. The seasons pass and the gun rusts and the brightly coloured costumes dull and rot and the leaves from all the trees round about fall on them, heap over them, cover them, and grass grows round them then starts growing out of them, through them, through ribs and eyeholes, then flowers appear in the grass, and when the costumes and the perishable parts have all rotted away or been eaten clean by creatures happy to have the sustenance, there's nothing left of them, the pantomime innocents or the man with the gun, but bones in grass, bones in flowers, the leafy branches of the ash tree above them. Which is what, in the end, is left of us all, whether we carry a gun while we're here or we don't. So. While we're here. I mean, while we're still here.

Daniel sat on the bench with his eyes closed for a moment. The moment got longer. It became less of a moment, more of a while.

Mr Gluck, Elisabeth said. Mr Gluck?

She jogged his elbow.

Ah. Yes. I was, I was – What was I?

You said the words, while we're here, Elisabeth said. You said it twice. While we're here. Then you stopped speaking.

Did I? Daniel said. While we're here. Well. While we're here, let's just always hold out hope for the person who says it.

Says what, Mr Gluck? Elisabeth said.

Sure you want war? Daniel said.

Elisabeth's mother is much cheerier this week, thank God. This is because she has received an email telling her she has been selected to appear on a TV programme called The Golden Gavel, where members of the public pit their wits against celebrities and antiques experts by trawling round antiques shops on a fixed budget and trying to buy the thing which in the end will raise the most money at auction. It's as if the Angel Gabriel has appeared at the door of her mother's life, kneeled down, bowed his head and told her: in a shop full of junk, somewhere among all the thousands and thousands of abandoned, broken, outdated, tarnished, sold-on, long-gone and forgotten things, there is something of much greater worth than anyone realizes, and the person we have chosen to

trust to unearth it from the dross of time and
history is you.

Elisabeth sits at the kitchen table while her
mother plays her an old episode of The Golden
Gavel to show her what they expect. Meanwhile she
thinks about her trip here, most of all about the
Spanish couple in the taxi queue at the station.

They'd clearly just arrived here on holiday, their
luggage round their feet. The people behind them
in the queue shouted at them. What they shouted at
them was to go home.

This isn't Europe, they shouted. Go back to Europe.

The people standing in front of the Spanish
people in the taxi queue were nice; they tried to
defuse it by letting the Spanish people take the next
taxi. All the same Elisabeth sensed that what was
happening in that one passing incident was a
fraction of something volcanic.

This is what shame feels like, she thinks.

Meanwhile on the screen it's still late spring and
the junk from the past is worth money. There is a
great deal of driving about in old cars from earlier
decades. There is a lot of stopping and worrying at
the side of the road about the smoke coming out of
the bonnets of the old cars.

Elisabeth tries to think of something to say to her
mother about The Golden Gavel.

I wonder which make of vintage car you'll get to
go in, she says.

No, because the members of the public don't get to, her mother says. It's only the celebrities and experts who get to do that. *They* arrive. *We're* already there at the shop waiting to meet them.

Why don't you get to go in a car? Elisabeth says. That's outrageous.

No point in devoting airtime to people who nobody knows from Adam driving about the place in old cars, her mother says.

Elisabeth notices how truly beautiful the cow parsley is at the sides of the backroads in the footage of The Golden Gavel, which is playing on catch-up, from an episode set in Oxfordshire and Gloucestershire, filmed, her mother tells her, last year. The cow parsley holds itself stately and poisonous in the air while the celebrities (Elisabeth has no idea who they are or why they're celebrities) maunder about. One sings pop songs from the 1970s and talks about when he owned a gold-painted Datsun. The other chats chummily about her days as an extra in Oliver! The vintage cars fume along through England; outside the car windows the passing cow parsley is tall, beaded with rain, strong, green. It is incidental. This incidentality is, Elisabeth finds herself thinking, a profound statement. The cow parsley has a language of its own, one that nobody on the programme or making the programme knows or notices is being spoken.

131

Elisabeth gets her phone out and makes a note. Maybe there's a lecture in this.

Then she remembers that probably pretty soon she won't have any job to give any lecture in anyway.

She puts her phone down on its lit front on the table. She thinks about the students she taught who graduate this week to all that debt, and now to a future in the past.

The cars on the TV programme draw up outside a warehouse in the countryside. There's a lot of getting out of the cars. At the door of the warehouse the celebrities and the experts meet the two ordinary people, who are wearing matching tracksuits to show that they're the ordinary people. Everyone shakes hands. Then they all set off, the celebrities, the experts and the ordinaries, in different directions round the warehouse.

One of the ordinary members of the public purchases an old till, or what the shop owner calls a vintage cash register, for £30. It doesn't work but its bright white and red buttons bristling off the curved chest of it remind her, the ordinary person says, of the regimental coat her grandfather wore when he was a cinema doorman in the 1960s. Cut to a celebrity who's spotted a cluster of charity boxes in the shapes of little life-sized figures – dogs and children – standing together at the door of the warehouse like a bunch of model villagers from the past, or from a sci-fi vision where past and future crash together. They're the boxes that used to sit outside shops for passers-by to put change into as they left or went into the shops. There is a bright pink girl with a teddybear; a dowdy looking boy mostly painted brown and holding what looks like an old sock; a bright red girl with the words thank-you carved into her chest and a brace on her leg; a spaniel with two puppies, their glass eyes pleading, little boxes round their necks, coin slots in the boxes, alternative coin slots in their heads.

An expert gets really excited. She explains to the camera that the brown clothed boy charity box, a Dr Barnardo's boy, is the most vintage of the set. She points out that the typography on the base the boy is standing on is pre-1960s, and that the little verse written on that base – Please Give, So He May Live – is itself a relic from a different time. Then she gives the camera a nod and a wink and tells it that if it were her she'd go for the spaniel regardless, because things in the shapes of dogs always do well at auction, and the brown clothed boy, though it has vintage status, is less likely to do as well as it ought to, unless the auction is an online one.

What they're not saying, her mother says, and maybe they're not saying it because they don't know it, is that those boxes came about because of real dogs back at the turn of the last century who worked going round places like railway stations with boxes hung round their necks for people to put pennies into. For charity.

Ah, Elisabeth says.

Those dog boxes, like that one there, were modelled on the real live creatures, her mother says. And furthermore. After the real live creatures died they would sometimes be stuffed by taxidermists and then placed back in the station or wherever, whichever public place they'd spent their working lives in. So you'd go to the station and there'd be Nip sitting there, or Rex, or Bob, dead, stuffed, but still with the box round his neck. And that, I'm certain, is where those dog-shaped charity boxes came from.

Elisabeth is faintly perturbed. She realizes this is because she likes to imagine her mother knows nothing much about anything.

Meanwhile the contestants on the screen spill out of the door excited about a set of mugs with Abraham Lincoln's Fiscal Policy printed on their sides. Outside the warehouse, in the green wastelands round about, there's a butterfly on the screen behind the heads of the presenters, small white waverer going from flowerhead to flowerhead.

And in astonishingly good nick, a celebrity is saying.

Hornsea, 1974, her mother says. Collector's dream.

Mid-70s, Yorkshire, the expert who's bought them says. Good clear Hornsea mark from the

American Presidents series on the base, the eagle mark. Hornsea started in 1949 after the war, went into receivership fifteen years ago, thriving in the 70s. Above all it's unusual to see seven of these together like this. A collector's dream.

See? her mother says.

Yes, but you've seen this episode already. So it's no big deal you knowing where they come from, Elisabeth says.

I know that. I meant I'm *learning*, her mother says. I meant I now *know* that that's what they are.

And I'd say that's the lot I'd be most worried about at auction, the first expert says in voiceover while the programme shows pictures of the chipped old charity boxes, one of the ordinary people rocking the red girl with the brace on her leg from side to side to see if there's any money still inside it.

I can't watch any more of this, Elisabeth says.

Why not? her mother says.

I mean I've seen enough, Elisabeth says. I've seen plenty. Thank you. It's very very exciting that you'll be on it.

Then her mother takes the laptop back to show Elisabeth one of the celebrities she'll be on the programme with.

Up comes a photograph of a woman in her sixties. Her mother waves the laptop in the air.

Look! she says. It's amazing, isn't it?

I have absolutely no idea who that is, Elisabeth says.

It's *Johnnie*! her mother says. From *Call Box Kids*!

The woman in her sixties was apparently a person on TV when Elisabeth's mother was a child.

I actually can't believe it, her mother is saying. I can't believe that I'm going to get to meet Johnnie. If only your grandmother was alive. If only I could tell her. If only I could tell my ten year old self. My ten year old self'd die with the excitement. Not just to get to meet. To get to be on a programme. With Johnnie.

Her mother turns the laptop towards her with a YouTube page up.

See? she says.

A girl of about fourteen in a checked shirt and with her hair in a ponytail is dancing a routine in a TV studio made to look like a London street, and the dancer she's dancing with is dressed as a phonebox, so that it literally looks like a public phonebox is dancing with the girl. The phonebox is rather rigid, as dancers go, and the girl has made herself rigid too and is doing steps to match the phonebox's. The girl is bright, warm, likeable, and the dancer inside the phonebox costume is making a pretty good attempt at dancing like a phonebox might. The street stops its business and everybody watches the dance. Then out of the open door of the box comes the receiver, up on its flex like a charmed snake, and the girl takes it, puts it to her head and the dance ends when she says the word: hello?

I actually remember seeing this very episode, Elisabeth's mother says. In our front room. When I was small.

Gosh, Elisabeth says.

Her mother watches it again. Elisabeth skims the day's paper on her phone to catch up on the usual huge changes there've been in the last half hour. She clicks on an article headed Look Into My Eyes: Leave. EU Campaign Consulted TV Hypnotist. She scrolls down and skims the screen. *The Power To Influence. I Can Make You Happy. Hypnotic Gastric Band. Helped produce social media ads. Are you concerned? Are you worried? Isn't it time? Being engrossed in TV broadcasts equally hypnotic. Facts don't work. Connect with people emotionally. Trump.* Her mother starts the forty years ago dance routine up one more time; the jaunty music begins again.

Elisabeth switches her phone off and goes through to the hall to get her coat.

I'm off out for a bit, she says.

Her mother, still in front of the screen, nods and waves without looking. Her eyes are bright with what are probably tears.

But it's a lovely day.

Elisabeth walks through the village, wondering if

those children-shaped charity boxes, since the dogs were modelled on real dogs, were also modelled on real beggars, small ones, child-beggars with callipers, boxes hung round their necks. Then she wonders if there was ever a plan afoot to taxiderm real children and stand them in stations.

As she passes the house with GO and HOME still written across it she sees that underneath this someone has added, in varying bright colours, WE ARE ALREADY HOME THANK YOU and painted a tree next to it and a row of bright red flowers underneath it. There are flowers, lots of real ones, in cellophane and paper, on the pavement outside the house, so it looks a bit like an accident has recently happened there.

She takes a photograph of the painted tree and flowers. Then she walks out of the village across the football pitch and out into the fields, thinking about the cow parsley, the painted flowers. The painting by Pauline Boty comes into her head, the one called With Love to Jean-Paul Belmondo. Maybe there's something in it whether she's got a job or not, something about the use of colour as language, the natural use of colour alongside the aesthetic use, the wild joyful brightness painted on the front of that house in a dire time, alongside the action of a painting like that one by Boty, in which a two-dimensional self is crowned with sensual colour, surrounded by orange and green and red so pure it's like they've come straight out of the tube on to the canvas, and not just by colour but by notional petals, the deep genital looking rose formation all over the hat on the head of the image of Belmondo as if to press him richly under at the same time as raise him richly up.

The cow parsley. The painted flowers. Boty's sheer unadulterated reds in the re-image-ing of the image. Put it together and what have you got? Anything useful?

She stops to make a note on her phone: *abandon and presence*, she writes.

It's the first time she's felt like herself for quite some time.

> *calm meets energy /*
> *artifice meets natural /*
> *electric energy /*
> *natural livewire /*

She looks up. She sees she's only yards from the fence across the common, the other kind of livewire.

The fence has doubled since she last saw it. Unless her eyes are deceiving her, it's now not just one fence but two in parallel.

It's true. Beyond the first layer of fence, about ten feet away from it, with a neat-flattened space in between the two fences, is another identical chainlink fence topped with the same foully frivolous looking razorwire. This other fence is electric-clipped too, and as she walks alongside them both the experience of the diamond-shaped wirework flashing next to her eyes is a bit epileptic.

Elisabeth takes a phone photo of it. Then she takes one or two images of the weed-life reappearing already through the churned-up mud round one of the metal posts.

She looks around. The weed and flower comeback is everywhere.

She follows the fenceline for half a mile or so before a black SUV truck rolling along in the flat space between the layers of fence catches up with her. It passes her and pulls up in front of her. The engine stops. When she draws level with the truck its window slides down. A man leans out. She nods a hello.

Fine day, she says.

You can't walk here, he says.

Yes I can, she says.

She nods to him again and smiles. She keeps walking. She hears the truck start up again behind her. When it draws level the driver keeps the engine dawdling, drives at the same pace as her walking. He leans out of the window.

This is private land, he says.

No it isn't, she says. It's common land. Common land is by definition not private.

She stops. The truck overshoots her. The man puts it into reverse.

Go back to the road, he calls out of the window as he reverses. Where's your car? You need to go back to where you left your car.

I can't do that, Elisabeth says.

Why not? the driver says.

I don't have a car, Elisabeth says.

She starts walking again. The driver revs his engine and drives beyond her. Several yards ahead of her he stops, cuts the engine and opens the truck door. He is standing beside the truck as she comes towards him.

You're in direct contravention, he says.

Of what? Elisabeth says. And whatever you say I'm in. Well. It looks from here like you're in prison.

He opens his top pocket and takes out a phone. He holds it up as if to take her picture or start filming her.

She points to the cameras on the fenceposts.

Don't you have enough footage of me already? she says.

Unless you leave the area immediately, he says, you'll be forcibly removed by security.

Are you *not* security, then? she says.

She points at the logo on the pocket he's taken the phone out of. It says SA4A.

And is that an approximation of the word *safer* or is it more like the word *sofa*? she says.

The SA4A man starts typing something on his phone.

This is your third warning, he says. You are now being warned for the last time that action will be taken against you unless you vacate the area immediately. You are unlawfully trespassing.

As opposed to lawfully trespassing? she says.

– still anywhere near the perimeter the next time I pass here –

Perimeter of what? she says.

She looks through at the fenced-off landscape and all she can see is landscape. There are no people. There are no buildings. There is just fence, then landscape.

– lead to legal charges being implemented against you, the man is saying, and may involve you being forcibly detained and your personal information and a sample of your DNA being taken and retained.

Prison for trees. Prison for gorse, for flies, for cabbage whites, for small blues. Oystercatcher detention centre.

What are the fences actually for? she says. Or aren't you allowed to tell me?

The man dead-eyes her. He keys something into his phone, then holds it up to get an image of her. She smiles in a friendly way, like you do when you're having your photo taken. Then she turns and starts walking again along the fenceline. She hears him phone somebody and say something, then get into his SUV and reverse it between the fences. She hears it head off in the opposite direction.

The nettles say nothing. The seeds at the tops of the grass stems say nothing. The little white flowers on the tops of their stalks, she doesn't know what they are but they're saying their fresh nothing.

The buttercups say it merrily. The gorse says it unexpectedly, a bright yellow nothing, smooth and soft and delicate against the mute green nothing of its barbs.

Back then at school a boy was hellbent on making Elisabeth, who was sixteen at this point, laugh. (He was hellbent on just making her, too, ha ha.) He was pretty cool. She liked him. His name was Mark Joseph and he played bass in a band that did anarchic cover versions of old stuff from back at the beginning of the 90s; he was also a computer genius who was ahead of everybody else, and this was back when most people still didn't know what a search engine was and everyone believed that the millennial new year would crash all the world's computers, about which Mark Joseph made a funny spoof and put it online, a photo of a veterinary surgery up the road from the school, caption underneath saying Click Here for Protection Against Millennium Pug.

Now he was following her about in school and trying to find ways of making her laugh.

He kissed her, at the school back gate. It
was nice.

Why don't you love me? he said three weeks later.

I'm already in love, Elisabeth said. It isn't possible
to be in love with more than one person.

A girl at college called Marielle Simi and
Elisabeth, when Elisabeth was eighteen, rolled about
on the floor of Elisabeth's hall of residence room
high on dope and laughing at the funny things that
backing singers sometimes sing in songs. Marielle
Simi played her an old song where the backing
singers have to sing the word onomatopoeia eight
times. Elisabeth played Marielle Simi a Cliff
Richard song in which the backing singers have to
sing the word sheep. They cried with laughter, then
Marielle Simi, who was French, put her arm round
Elisabeth and kissed her. It was nice.

Why? she said, months later. I don't get it. I don't
understand. It's so good.

I just can't lie, Elisabeth said. I love the sex. I love
being with you. It's great. But I have to be truthful.
I can't lie about it.

Who is he? Marielle Simi said. An ex? Is he still
around? Are you still seeing him? Or is it a her? Is it
a woman? Have you been seeing her or him the
whole time you've been seeing me?

It isn't that kind of relationship, Elisabeth said. It
isn't even the least bit physical. It never has been.
But it's love. I can't pretend it isn't.

You are using this as denial, Marielle Simi said. You're putting it between yourself and your real feelings so that you don't have to feel.

Elisabeth shrugged.

I feel plenty, she said.

Elisabeth, who was twenty one, met Tom MacFarlane at her graduation. She was graduating in history of art (morning), he was business studies (afternoon). Tom and Elisabeth had been together for six years. He'd moved into her rented flat for five so far of those years. They were thinking of making their relationship permanent. They were talking marriage, mortgage.

One morning when he was putting breakfast things out on the kitchen table Tom asked out of nowhere, who's Daniel?

Daniel? Elisabeth said.

Daniel, Tom said again.

Do you mean Mr Gluck? she said.

I've no idea, Tom said. Who's Mr Gluck?

Old neighbour of my mother's, Elisabeth said. He lived next door when I was a kid. I haven't seen him for years. Literally years. Ages. Why? Has something happened? Did my mother phone? Has something happened to Daniel?

You said his name in your sleep, Tom said.

Did I? When? Elisabeth said.

Last night. It's not the first time. You quite often say it in your sleep, Tom said.

Elisabeth was fourteen. She and Daniel were walking where the canal met the countryside, where the path peels away and goes off up through to the woods on the curve of the hill. It was suddenly freezing though it was only quite early in autumn. The rain was coming, she could see it when they got to the top of the hill, it was moving across the landscape like someone was shading in the sky with a pencil.

Daniel was out of breath. He didn't usually get this out of breath.

I don't like it when the summer goes and the autumn comes, she said.

Daniel took her by the shoulders and turned her round. He didn't say anything. But all across the landscape down behind them it was still sunlit blue and green.

She looked up at him showing her how the summer was still there.

Nobody spoke like Daniel.

Nobody didn't speak like Daniel.

It was the end of a winter; this one was the winter of 2002–3. Elisabeth was eighteen. It was February. She had gone down to London to march in the protest. Not In Her Name. All across the country people had done the same thing and millions more people had all across the world.

On the Monday after, she wandered through the city; strange to be walking streets where life was going on as normal, traffic and people going their usual backwards and forwards along streets that had had no traffic, had felt like they'd belonged to the two million people from their feet on the pavement all the way up to sky because of something to do with truth, when she'd walked the exact same route only the day before yesterday.

That was the Monday she unearthed an old red hardback catalogue in an art shop on Charing

Cross Road. It was cheap, £3. It was in the reduced books bin.

It was of an exhibition a few years ago. Pauline Boty, 1960s Pop Art painter.

Pauline who?

A female British Pop Art painter?

Really?

This was interesting to Elisabeth, who'd been studying art history as one of her subjects at college and had been having an argument with her tutor, who'd told her that categorically there had never been such a thing as a female British Pop artist, not one of any worth, which is why there were none recorded as more than footnotes in British Pop Art history.

The artist had made collages, paintings, stained glass work and stage sets. She had had quite a life story. She'd not just been a painter, she'd also done theatre and TV work as an actress, had chaperoned Bob Dylan round London before anyone'd heard of Bob Dylan, had been on the radio telling listeners what it was like to be a young woman in the world right then and had nearly been cast in a film in a role that Julie Christie got instead.

She'd had everything ahead of her in swinging London, and then she'd died, at the age of twenty eight, of cancer. She'd gone to the doctor because she was pregnant and they'd spotted the cancer. She'd refused an abortion, which meant she couldn't have radiotherapy; it would hurt the child. She'd given birth and she'd died four months after.

Malignant thymoma is what it said in the list of things under the word Chronology at the back of the catalogue.

It was a sad story, and nothing like the paintings, which were so witty and joyous and full of unexpected colour and juxtapositions that Elisabeth, flicking through the catalogue, realized that she was smiling. The painter's last painting had been of a huge and beautiful female arse, nothing else, framed by a jovial proscenium arch like it was filling the whole stage of a theatre. Underneath, in bright red, was a word in huge and rambunctious looking capitals.

BUM.

Elisabeth laughed out loud.

What a way to go.

The artist's paintings were full of images of people of the time, Elvis, Marilyn, people from politics. There was a photograph of a now-missing painting with the famous image of the woman who caused the Scandal scandal, whose sitting nude and backwards on a designer chair had had something to do with politics at the time.

Then Elisabeth held the catalogue open at a page with a particular painting on it.

It was called Untitled (Sunflower Woman) c.1963.

It was of a woman on a bright blue background.

Her body was a collage of painted images. A man with a machine gun pointing at the person looking at the picture formed her chest. A factory formed her arm and shoulder.

A sunflower filled her torso.

An exploding airship made her crotch.

An owl.

Mountains.

Coloured zigzags.

At the back of the book was a black and white reproduction of a collage. It had a large hand holding a small hand, which was holding the large hand back.

Down at the bottom of the picture there were two ships in a sea and a small boat filled with people.

Elisabeth went to the British Library periodicals room and sat at a table with Vogue, September 1964. *FEATURES 9 Spotlight 92 Paola, paragon of princesses 110 Living doll: Pauline Boty interviewed by Nell Dunn 120 Girls in their married bliss, by Edna O'Brien.* Alongside adverts for the bright red Young Jaeger look-again coat, the Goya Golden Girl Beauty Puff and the bandeau bra and pantie girdle cut like briefs to leave you feeling free all over, was: *Pauline Boty, blonde, brilliant, 26. She has been married for a year and her husband is inordinately proud of her achievements, boasts that she makes a lot of money painting and* acting. *She has found by experience that she is in a world where female emancipation is a password and not a fact – she is beautiful, therefore she should not be clever.*

The full-page photo, by David Bailey, was a large close-up of Boty's face with a tiny doll's face, the other way up, just behind her.

P.B. *I find that I have a fantasy image. It's that I really like making other people happy, which is probably egotistical, because they think 'What a lovely girl', you know. But it's also that I don't want people to touch me. I don't mean physically particularly, though it's that as well. So I always like to feel that I'm sort of floating by and just occasionally being there, seeing them. I'm very inclined to play a role that someone sets for me, particularly when I first meet people. One of the reasons I married Clive was because he really did accept me as a human being, a person with a mind.*

N.D. *Men think of you just as a pretty girl you mean?*

P.B. *No. They just find it embarrassing when you start talking. Lots of women are intellectually more clever than lots of men. But it's difficult for men to accept the idea.*

N.D. *If you start talking about ideas they just think you're putting it on?*

P.B. Not that you're putting it on. They just find it
slightly embarrassing that you're not doing the
right thing.

Elisabeth photocopied the pages in the magazine.
She took the Pauline Boty exhibition catalogue to
college and put it on her tutor's desk.
Oh, right. Boty, the tutor said.
He shook his head.
Tragic story, he said.
Then he said, they're pretty dismissible. Poor
paintings. Not very good. She was quite Julie
Christie. Very striking girl. There's a film of her,
Ken Russell, and she's a bit eccentric in it if I
remember rightly, dresses in a top hat, miming
along to Shirley Temple, I mean attractive and so
on, but pretty execrable.
Where can I find that film? Elisabeth said.
I've absolutely no idea, the tutor said. She was
gorgeous. But not a painter of anything more than
minor interest. She stole everything of any note in
her work from Warhol and Blake.
What about the way she uses images as images?
Elisabeth said.
Oh God, everybody and his dog was doing that
then, the tutor said.
What about everybody and *her* dog?
Elisabeth said.
I'm sorry? the tutor said.

154

What about this? Elisabeth said.

She opened the catalogue at a page with two paintings reproduced side by side.

One was of a painting of images of ancient and modern men. Above, there was a blue sky with a US airforce plane in it. Below, there was a smudged colour depiction of the shooting of Kennedy in the car in Dallas, between black and white images of Lenin and Einstein. Above the head of the dying president were a matador, a deep red rose, some smiling men in suits, a couple of the Beatles.

The other picture was of a fleshy strip of images superimposed over a blue/green English landscape vista, complete with a little Palladian structure. Inside the superimposed strip were several images of part-naked women in lush and coquettish porn magazine poses. But at the centre of these coy poses was something unadulterated, pure and blatant, a woman's naked body full-frontal, cut off at the head and the knees.

The tutor shook his head.

I'm not seeing anything new here, he said.

He cleared his throat.

There are lots and lots of highly sexualized images throughout Pop Art, he said.

What about the titles? Elisabeth said.

(The titles of the paintings were It's a Man's World I and It's a Man's World II.)

The tutor had gone a ruddy red colour at the face.

Is there, was there, anything else like this being painted by a woman at the time? Elisabeth said.

The tutor shut the catalogue. He cleared his throat again.

Why should we imagine that gender matters here? the tutor said.

That's actually my question too, Elisabeth said. In fact, I came to see you today to change my dissertation title. I'd like to work on the representation of representation in Pauline Boty's work.

You can't, the tutor said.

Why can't I? Elisabeth said.

There's not nearly enough material available on Pauline Boty, the tutor said.

I think there is, Elisabeth said.

There's next to no critical material, he said.

That's one of the reasons I think it'd be a particularly good thing to do, Elisabeth said.

I'm your dissertation supervisor, the tutor said, and I'm telling you, there isn't, and it isn't. You're going off down a rarefied cul-de-sac here. Do I make myself clear?

Then I'd like to apply to be moved to a new supervisor, Elisabeth said. Do I do that with you, or do I go to the Admin office?

A year on from then, Elisabeth went home for the

Easter holidays. It was when her mother was thinking of moving, maybe to the coast. Elisabeth listened to the options and looked at the house details her mother had been sent by estate agents in Norfolk and Suffolk.

After the right amount of time talking about houses had passed, Elisabeth asked after Daniel.

Won't have any help in the house, her mother said. Won't have meals on wheels. Won't let anyone make him a cup of anything or do his washing or change his old bed. The house smells pretty strong, but if anyone goes round there offering anything, offering to help out, he makes you sit down, then makes you a cup of tea himself, won't hear of anyone even doing that for him. Ninety if he's a day. He's not up to it. I had to fish a dead beetle out of the last cup of tea he made me.

I'll just nip round and see him, Elisabeth said.

Oh, hello, Daniel said. Come in. What you reading?

Elisabeth waited for him to make her the cup of tea. Then she got the exhibition catalogue she'd found in London out of her bag and put it on the table.

When I was small, Mr Gluck, she said, I don't know if you remember, but when we went on walks you sometimes described paintings to me, and the thing is, I think I've finally managed to see some of them.

157

Daniel put his glasses on. He opened the catalogue. He flushed, then he went pale.

Oh yes, he said.

He leafed through the pages. His face lit up. He nodded. He shook his head.

Aren't they fine? he said.

I think they're really brilliant, Elisabeth said. Really outstanding. Also really thematically and technically interesting.

Daniel turned a picture towards her, blue and red abstracts, blacks and golds and pinks in circles and curves.

I remember this one very clearly, he said.

I wondered, Mr Gluck, Elisabeth said. Because of our conversations, and you knowing them so well, the pictures. I mean they've been missing for decades. They've just been rediscovered, really. And no one in the art world knows about them, except, from what I can gather, from people who knew her in person. I went and asked about her at the gallery where they showed these pictures, like seven or eight years back, and I met this woman who knew someone who used to know Boty a bit, and she told me that the woman she knows still sometimes just finds herself in floods of tears, even nearly forty years later, whenever she remembers her friend. So, I was wondering. It struck me. That maybe you knew Boty too.

Well well, he said. Look at that.

He was still looking at the blue abstract called Gershwin.

I never knew till now she called it that, he said.

And when you look at the photos of her, Elisabeth said. And she was so incredibly beautiful. And what happened to her in her life is so sad, and then the sad things that happened after her own sad death, to her husband, and then to her daughter, just tragedy after tragedy, so unbearably sad that –

Daniel put one hand up to tell her to stop, then the other, both hands up and flat.

Silence.

He went back to the book on the table between them. He turned the page to the one with the woman made of flames, and the bright yellow abstract opposite it, reds, pinks, blues and whites.

Look at that, he said.

He nodded.

They truly are something, he said.

He turned all the pages, one after the other. Then he shut the book and put it back on the table. He looked up at Elisabeth.

There have been very many men and women in my life whom I hoped might, whom I wanted to, love me, he said. But I only, myself, ever, loved, in that way, just once. And it wasn't a person I fell in love with. No, not a person at all.

He tapped the cover of the book.

It is possible, he said, to be in love not with

someone but with their eyes. I mean, with how eyes that aren't yours let you see where you are, who you are.

Elisabeth nodded as if she understood.

Not a person.

Yes, and the 60s zeitgeist, she said, is –

Daniel, his hand up, stopped her again.

We have to hope, Daniel was saying, that the people who love us and who know us a little bit will in the end have seen us truly. In the end, not much else matters.

But a coldness was shifting all through her body, wiping her into a clarity much like a soapy window by a window cleaner from top to base with a rubber blade.

He nodded, more to the room than to Elisabeth.

It's the only responsibility memory has, he said. But, of course, memory and responsibility are strangers. They're foreign to each other. Memory always goes its own way quite regardless.

Elisabeth will have looked like she was listening, but inside her head there was the high-pitched hiss, the blood going round inside her making itself heard above any and every other thing.

Not a person.
Daniel does not –
Daniel has never –
Daniel has never known –

She drank the tea. She excused herself. She left the book on the table.

He came hobbling after her into the hall holding it out to her as she was unsnibbing the front door.

I left it on purpose, for you, she said. I thought you might like it. I won't need it. I've handed in my dissertation.

He shook his old head.

You keep it, he said.

She heard the door shutting behind her.

**It was one of the days of a week in one of the
seasons in one of the years,** maybe 1949, maybe
1950, 1951, in any case sometime around then.

Christine Keeler, who'd be famous just over a
decade later, being one of the witting/unwitting
agents of the huge changes in the class and sexual
mores of the 1960s, was a small girl out playing
down by the river with some of the boys.

They unearthed a metal thing. It will have been
round at one end and pointed at the other.

A small bomb will have been about as big as their
upper bodies. They knew it was a bomb. So they
decided they'd take it home to show to the father of
one of the boys. He'd presumably been in the army.
He'd know what to do with it.

It was mucky from being buried so they cleaned
it up maybe, with wet grass and jumper sleeves,

first. Then they took turns carrying it back to their street. A couple of times they dropped it. When they did they ran away like crazy in case it went off.

They got it to the boy's house. The boy's father came out to see what all the kids outside the house wanted.

Oh dear God.

The RAF came. They got everybody out of the houses all up and down the street, then everybody out of the houses in all the streets around the street.

Next day those kids got their names in the local paper.

That story comes from one of the books she wrote about her life. Here's another. When she wasn't yet ten years old, Christine Keeler was sent to live in a convent for a while. One of the bedtime stories the nuns told all the little girls there was about a little boy called Rastus.

Rastus is in love with a little white girl. But the little white girl gets ill, and it looks like she's going to die. Someone tells Rastus that she'll be dead by the time the leaves have fallen off the tree at the front of her house. So Rastus collects up all the shoelaces he can find. Maybe he also unravels his jumper and cuts the unravelled wool into pieces. He's going to need a lot of pieces. He climbs the tree outside the girl's house. He ties the leaves on to the branches.

But one night a really wild wind blows all the leaves off the tree.

(Forty years before Christine Keeler was born, but presumably at a time when a lot of those nuns who apparently told stories like this one to the little girls in their care were growing up or were young adults, Rastus was a name popular in blackface minstrel shows. It became a character-name, a racist shorthand for someone black, in early films, in turn of the century fiction, across all the forms of early media entertainment.

In the States, from the start of the century till the mid-20s, a black figure named Rastus was used to advertise Cream of Wheat breakfast cereal. He wore a chef's hat and jacket in all the photographs of him and in one particular illustration an old and white-bearded black man with a stick stops to look at a picture of Rastus on a poster advertising *Cream of Wheat For Your Breakfast* and the caption underneath reads: *'Ah reckon as how he's de bes' known man in de worl.'*

In the mid-20s, Cream of Wheat replaced the character-name Rastus with the character-name Frank L White, though the illustrations on the posters and in the adverts stayed much the same. Frank L White was a real man whose facial image, in a photograph taken around 1900 when he was a chef in Chicago, became Cream of Wheat's standard advertising image. It's not recorded anywhere whether White was ever paid for the use of his image.

He died in 1938.

It took another seventy years for his grave to be officially marked with a stone.

Back to Christine Keeler.)

There's another story she tells about herself in the couple of books written by her and her ghostwriters.

This one is from another time in her childhood. It's about the day she found a fieldmouse. She brought it home as a pet.

The man she called Dad killed it. He did this by standing on it, presumably as she watched.

Same as all the other times, Daniel is sleeping.

To the people here he is maybe just another shape in a bed they keep serviceably clean. They are still rehydrating him, though they've let Elisabeth know they'll want to talk to her mother about whether to cease rehydrating or not.

I want you, my mother and I both completely want you, especially my mother does, to keep rehydrating him, Elisabeth said when they asked.

The Maltings Care Providers plc are very keen to have a conference with her mother, the receptionist tells her when she arrives.

I'll tell her, Elisabeth says. She'll be in touch.

The receptionist says they'd like to flag up as gently as possible with her mother their concern that payment provision for the accommodation and care package for Mr Gluck at The Maltings

Care Providers plc is shortly going to fall into default.

We'll definitely be in touch about it really really soon, Elisabeth says.

The receptionist goes back to her iPad, on which she's paused a crime serial on catch-up. Elisabeth watches the screen for a moment or two. A woman dressed as a policewoman is being run over by a young man in a car. He runs over her on the road, then he does it again. Then he does it again.

Elisabeth goes to Daniel's room and sits down at the side of the bed.

They are definitely still rehydrating him.

One of his hands has come out from under the covers and gone to his mouth. It has the rehydration needle taped into the back of it and the tube taped along the side of it. (A thin taut string breaks in Elisabeth's chest at seeing the tape and the needle.) Daniel touches, still deep in the sleep, his top lip, but lightly, brushingly, like someone would if he were clearing away breadcrumbs or croissant crumbs. It's as if he's feeling, in the least conspicuous way, to test or to make sure he still has a mouth, or that his fingers can still feel. Then the hand disappears back down inside the covers.

Elisabeth sneaks a look at the chart clipped on to the end of Daniel's bed, the graphs with the temperature and blood pressure readings on them.

The chart says on its first page that Daniel is a hundred and one years old.

Elisabeth laughs to herself.

(Her mother: *How old are you, Mr Gluck?*

Daniel: *Nowhere near as old as I intend to be, Mrs Demand.*)

Today he looks like a Roman senator, his sleeping head noble, his eyes shut and blank as a statue, his eyebrows mere moments of frost.

It is a privilege, to watch someone sleep, Elisabeth tells herself. It is a privilege to be able to witness someone both here and not here. To be included in someone's absence, it is an honour, and it asks quiet. It asks respect.

No. It is awful.

It is fucking awful.

It is awful to be on the literal other side of his eyes.

Mr Gluck, she says.

She says it quiet, confidential, down near his left ear.

Two things. I'm not sure what to do about the money they need you to pay here. I wonder if there's something you'd like me to do about it. And the other thing. They want to know about rehydrating you. Do you want to be rehydrated?

Do you need to go?

Do you want to stay?

Elisabeth stops speaking. She sits up again away from Daniel's sleeping head.

Daniel breathes in. Then he breathes out. Then, for a long time, there's no breath. Then it starts again.

One of the care assistants comes in. She starts wiping at the bedrail then the windowsill with cleaning stuff.

He's quite some gentleman, she says with her back to Elisabeth.

She turns round.

What did he do in his good long life? After the war, I mean.

Elisabeth realizes she has no idea.

He wrote songs, she says. And he helped out a lot with my childhood. When I was little.

We were all amazed, the care assistant says, when he told us about in the war, when they interned them. Him being English really but going in there with his old father the German, even though he could have stayed outside if he'd chosen. And how he tried to get his sister over, but they said no.

In-breath.

Out-breath.

Long pause.

Did he tell you that? Elisabeth says.

The care assistant hums a tune. She wipes the doorhandle, then the edges of the door. She takes a long stick made of white plastic with a white cotton rectangle on the end of it and she wipes the top of the door and round the lampshade.

He's never talked about any of that, not to us,
Elisabeth says.

Family for you, the care assistant says. Easier to
talk to someone you don't know. He and I had
many a chat, before he went off. One day he said a
very fair thing. When the state is not kind, he said.
We were talking about the vote, it was coming up,
I've thought about it a lot, since. Then the people
are fodder, he said. Wise man, your grandad.
Clever man.

The care assistant smiles at her.

It's a lovely thing you do, coming to read to him.
A thoughtful thing.

The care assistant wheels her little trolley out.
Elisabeth watches her broad back as she goes, and
the way the material of her overall stretches tight
across it and under her arms.

I know nothing, nothing really, about anyone.

Maybe nobody does.

In-breath.

Out-breath.

Long pause.

She closes her eyes. Dark.

She opens her eyes again.

She opens her book at random. She starts to
read, from where she's opened it, but this time
out loud, to Daniel: *His sisters, the nymphs of
the spring, mourned for him, and cut off their hair
in tribute to their brother. The wood nymphs*

mourned him too, and Echo sang her refrain to their lament.

The pyre, the tossing torches, and the bier, were now being prepared, but his body was nowhere to be found. Instead of his corpse, they discovered a flower with a circle of white petals round a yellow centre.

I'm thirteen years old in that one, her mother was saying. Seaside holiday. We went every year. That's my mother. My father.

The next door neighbour was in their front room.

It was just after Elisabeth had told him she had a sister. Now she was worried the neighbour would give the game away and ask her mother where the other daughter was.

So far he hadn't said anything about it.

He was looking at the family photographs of her mother on the wall in the front room.

Now those, he was saying, are completely fantastic.

Her mother hadn't just made coffee, she'd made it in the good mugs.

Forgive me, Mrs Demand, the neighbour said. I mean, the photos are lovely. But the tin signs. The real thing.

173

The what, Mr Gluck? her mother said.

She put the mugs on the table and came over to have a look.

Call me Daniel, please, the neighbour said.

He pointed at the picture.

Oh, her mother said. Those. Yes.

There were hoardings advertising ice lollies in one of the old photographs, behind her mother as a child. This was what they were talking about.

6d, her mother said. I was still a very small child when decimalization came in. But I remember the heavy pennies. The half crowns.

She was speaking in a slightly too loud way. The neighbour, Daniel, didn't seem to notice or mind.

Look at that wedge of dark pink on the bright pink, Daniel said. Look at the blue, the way the shadow deepens there where the colour changes.

Yes, her mother said. Zoom. Fab.

Daniel sat down beside the cat.

What's her name? he said to Elisabeth.

Barbra, Elisabeth said. After the singer.

The singer her mother loves, her mother said.

Daniel winked at Elisabeth and said, but quietly, down towards her like it was a secret so her mother, who'd gone to the CD shelf now and was going through the CDs, wouldn't hear, as if he didn't want her to know,

after the singer who once, believe it or not, sang a song I wrote the words for, in concert. I was very handsomely paid. But she never recorded it. I'd be a trillionaire, had she. Rich enough to time-travel.

Can you sing? Elisabeth said.

Not at all, Daniel said.

Would you actually *like* to time-travel? she said. If you could, I mean, and time travel was a real thing?

Very much indeed, Daniel said.

Why? Elisabeth said.

Time travel *is* real, Daniel said. We do it all the time. Moment to moment, minute to minute.

He opened his eyes wide at Elisabeth. Then he put his hand in his pocket, took out a twenty pence piece, held it in front of Barbra the cat. He did something with his other hand and the coin disappeared! He made it disappear!

The song about love being an easy chair filled the room. Barbra the cat was still looking in disbelief at Daniel's empty hand. She put both paws up, held the hand, put her nose into it to look for the missing coin. Her cat face was full of amazement.

See how it's deep in our animal nature, Daniel said. Not to see what's happening right in front of our eyes.

October's a blink of the eye. The apples weighing down the tree a minute ago are gone and the tree's leaves are yellow and thinning. A frost has snapped millions of trees all across the country into brightness. The ones that aren't evergreen are a combination of beautiful and tawdry, red orange gold the leaves, then brown, and down.

The days are unexpectedly mild. It doesn't feel that far from summer, not really, if it weren't for the underbite of the day, the lacy creep of the dark and the damp at its edges, the plants calm in the folding themselves away, the beads of the condensation on the webstrings hung between things.

On the warm days it feels wrong, so many leaves falling.

But the nights are cool to cold.

The spiders in the sheds and the houses are guarding their egg sacs in the roof corners.

The eggs for the coming year's butterflies are tucked on the undersides of the grassblades, dotting the dead looking stalks on the wasteland, camouflaged invisible on the scrubby looking bushes and twigs.

3

Here's an old story so new that it's still in the middle of happening, writing itself right now with no knowledge of where or how it'll end. An old man is sleeping in a bed in a care facility on his back with his head pillow-propped. His heart is beating and his blood's going round his body, he's breathing in then out, he is asleep and awake and he's nothing but a torn leaf scrap on the surface of a running brook, green veins and leaf-stuff, water and current, Daniel Gluck taking leaf of his senses at last, his tongue a broad green leaf, leaves growing through the sockets of his eyes, leaves thrustling (very good word for it) out of his ears, leaves tendrilling down through the caves of his nostrils and out and round till he's swathed in foliage, leafskin, relief.

And here he is now, sitting next to his little sister!

But his little sister's name escapes him for the
moment. This is surprising. It's one of the words
he's held dear his whole life. Never mind. Here she
is next to him. He turns his head and she's there.
It's unbearably lovely to see her! She's sitting next to
the painter, the one that turned him copiously
down, well, that's life, he can even smell the scent
the painter wore, Oh! de London, bright, sweet,
woody, when he first knew her, then she got older
and more serious and it was Rive Gauche, he can
smell it too.

They're both, his sister and the painter, ignoring
him. Nothing new there. They're conversing with a
man he doesn't recognize, young, long hair, earnest
looking, wearing old clothes from the past or
maybe from a heaped-up pile of old costumes below
a stage in a theatre; the man straightens a wide cuff
at his wrist, he is speaking about how he likes a
stubble field *better than the chilly green of the
spring*, he says. His sister and the painter are
agreeing with him and Daniel finds himself
becoming a bit jealous, *stubble-plain looks warm*,
the young man turns to the painter, *in the same
way some pictures look warm*, the painter nods,
without my eyes, she says, bright and glittering the
pieces of her voice, *I don't exist*.

He tries to get his little sister's attention.

He nudges her elbow.

She ignores him.

But there's something he's been waiting to say to his little sister, he's wanted to for more than sixty years, since he thought it, and every time he's thought it again since, he's wished she were alive even just for half a minute. How interesting she'll find it. (He wants her to be impressed, too, that he's thought it at all.) Kandinsky, he says. Paul Klee, I'm sure. They're making the first pictures ever made of it. A whole new landscape painting. They're picturing the view from the inside of the eye, but precisely when the migraine is happening to it!

His little sister is prone to migraines.

I mean, all the bright yellow, the pink and black triangles pulsating along the curves and the lines.

His little sister sighs.

Now he is sitting on the windowsill of her room. She is twelve. He's seventeen, much older than she is. So why does he feel so junior? His little sister is brilliant. She is at her desk deep in a book, half-opened books all over her desk, all over the floor and the bed. She likes to read, she reads all the time, and she prefers to be reading several things at once, she says it gives endless perspective and dimension. They've been at each other's throats all summer long. He and his father are off back tomorrow, school, England, where he also doesn't quite belong. He is trying to be nice. She is ignoring him. The nicer he is, the more she despises him. This being despised by her is new. Last year and all the years before it he was her hero. Last year she still liked it when he told the jokes, made the coins vanish. This year she rolls her eyes. The city, old as it is, is also somehow new and strange. Nothing's different, but everything is. It's scented by the same old trees. It is summer-jovial. But this year its joviality is a kind of open threat.

Yesterday she caught him in tears in his room. She opened the door. He ordered her away. She didn't go. She stood in the doorway instead. What's wrong? she said. Are you scared? He told her no. He told her a blatant lie. He told her he had been thinking about Mozart and how young and broken he'd been when he died, and how light the music, and that this had moved him to tears. I see, she said in the doorway. She knew perfectly well he was lying. Not that Mozart isn't capable of making him cry, and often does, with the high sweet notes which feel, though he'd never say such an unsayable out loud thing to anyone, let alone his little sister, like tiny orgasms. But truly? It wasn't what was making him cry right then. Come on, summer brother (it's what she's taken to calling him, like he's not always her brother, he's just her brother in the summer), she said drumming her fingers on the wood of the door panelling. That's nothing to cry about.

Today she looks up from the desk and feigns surprise that he's still here.

I'm just going, he says.

But he stays sitting there on the windowsill.

Well, if you're going to sit there emanating such melancholy, she says, can you make yourself more useful? Instead of sick?

Sick? he says.

Transit gloria mundi, she says. Ha ha.

She is unbearable. He hates her.

Don't just sit there like an unstrung puppet, she says. Be here. Do something. Tell me something.

Tell you what? he says.

I don't know, she says. I don't care. Anything. Tell me what you're reading.

Oh, I'm reading so many things, he says.

She knows he's reading nothing. She's the one who reads, not him.

Tell me something from one of the many things you're reading, she says.

She is trying to humiliate him, first for feeling, second for not reading like she does.

But there's a story they were made to read, school, French lessons. That'll do.

I've actually been reading, he says, the world-renowned story of the ancient old man who happens to be in possession of a magic goatskin. But being so old, nearly as old as legend itself, he's going to die soon –

Because human beings can't be legends, being mortal, she says.

Uh huh, he says.

She laughs.

And he wants to pass on the magic goatskin to someone else, he says.

Why does he? she says.

His mind goes blank. He has no idea why.

So the magic won't get wasted, he says. So, uh, so that –

Where did he get the magic goatskin in the first place? she says.

He has no idea. He wasn't really listening in the class.

Was there once a magic goat? she says. On the ledges of a cliff? One that could jump any height and any angle and still land on its delicate little hoofs? Or did it have to be skinned and then the skin became magic *after* the sacrifice, because of the sacrifice?

She doesn't even know the story and she's made up a better one than the one he's trying to remember.

Well? she says.

The magic goatskin, he says, was, well, it was the cover on one of the ancient old man's oldest most powerful books of magic, and therefore had been saturated in magic for hundreds and hundreds of years. So he removed the skin from it precisely, in fact, so that he could pass it on.

Why doesn't he *therefore* pass on *precisely in fact* the whole book? his little sister says.

She's turned at her desk towards him, her face half mockery, half affection.

I don't know, he says. All I know is that he decided to pass it on. So he, uh, finds a young man to pass it on to.

Why a young man? his little sister says. Why doesn't he choose a young woman?

Look, he says. I'm just telling you what I read. And the old man said to the young man, here. Have this magic goatskin. Treat it with respect. It is very very powerful. What you do to get it to work is, you put your hand on it, and you make a wish. And then your wish comes true. But what he didn't tell the young man was that every time you wish on the magic goatskin, the magic goatskin gets smaller, it shrinks in size, in a small way or a big way, depending on how small or how vast the wish you wish on it is. And so the young man wished, and his wish came true, and he did it again and his wish came true. And he went through his life full of good fortune wishing on the magic goatskin. But the day came when the magic goatskin had shrunk so small it was smaller than the palm of his hand. So he wished for it to be bigger, and when he did it grew bigger, bigger, bigger, every bit as big as the world, and when it reached the size of the world it disappeared, thin air.

His little sister rolls her eyes.

And that's when the young man, now a slightly

older man, though not as old, I don't think, as the original ancient old man, died, he says.

His little sister sighs.

Is that it? she says.

Well, there's other bits of it that I haven't remembered, he says. But yes, that's the gist of it.

Fine, she says.

She comes over to the window and kisses him on the cheek.

Thank you very much for telling me the story of the magic foreskin, she says.

He doesn't hear what she's said until a moment after she's said it. When he does he blushes to the roots of his hair. His whole body blushes. She sees him redden and she smiles.

Because I'm not meant to say that word, am I? she says. Even though that's what the story's really about. Even though hundreds of years of disguise are meant to keep me away from what the world's stories are really all about. Well, foreskin. Foreskin foreskin foreskin.

She dances round the room shouting the word he could hardly say in her presence out loud himself.

She is mad.

But she is uncannily right about that story.

She is brilliant.

She is a whole new level of the word true.

She is dangerous and shining.

She comes over to the window and pushes it

wider. She shouts into the street, into the sky (in English, though, thank God), *foreskins come and foreskins go! But Mozart lasts forever!* Then she skips back over to her seat at the desk, picks up the book she is reading and starts back into the middle of it again like nothing has happened.

He waits a moment then glances out and down to the street. A lady with a little dog has stopped and is standing there looking up, hand shielding her eyes; apart from that the street continues as ever, with no idea that his little sister is *that* mad, *that* brave, *that* clever, *that* wild and *that* calm, and that he now knows for sure that when she grows up she's going to be a great force in the world, an important thinker, a changer of things, someone to be reckoned with.

Summer brother.

Old man in a bed in a care facility.

Little sister.

Never more than twenty, twenty one.

There are no pictures left of her. The photos at their mother's house? long burnt, lost, gone, street litter.

But he has some pages, still, of the letters from when she was nursing their mother. She is eighteen. The clever forward-slope of her.

It's a question of how we regard our situations, dearest Dani, how we look and see where we are, and how we choose, if we can, when we are seeing

*undeceivedly, not to despair and, at the same time,
how best to act. Hope is exactly that, that's all it is,
a matter of how we deal with the negative acts
towards human beings by other human beings in
the world, remembering that they and we are all
human, that nothing human is alien to us, the foul
and the fair, and that most important of all we're
here for a mere blink of the eyes, that's all. But in
that Augenblick there's either a benign wink or a
willing blindness, and we have to know we're
equally capable of both, and to be ready to be
above and beyond the foul even when we're up to
our eyes in it. So it's important – and here I
acknowledge directly the kind and charming and
mournful soul of my dear brother whom I know
so well – not to waste the time, our time, when
we have it.*

Dearest Dani.

What has he done with the time?

A few trivial rhymes.

There was nothing else for it, really.

Plus, he ate well, when the rhymes brought in the
money.

Autumn mellow. Autumn yellow. He can
remember every word of that stupid song. But he
can't remember,

dear God, he can't.

Excuse me, dear God, can I trouble you to
remind me of my little sister's name?

Not that he thinks there's a God. In fact he knows there isn't. But just in case there's such a thing:

Please, remind me, her name, again.

Sorry, the silence says. Can't help you.

Who's that?

(Silence.)

Who's there?

(Silence.)

God?

Not exactly.

Well, who?

Where do I start? I'm the butterfly antenna. I'm the chemicals that paint's made of. I'm the person dead at the water's edge. I'm the water. I'm the edge. I'm skin cells. I'm the smell of disinfectant. I'm that thing they rub against your mouth to moisten it, can you feel it? I'm soft. I'm hard. I'm glass. I'm sand. I'm a yellow plastic bottle. I'm all the plastics in the seas and in the guts of all the fishes. I'm the fishes. I'm the seas. I'm the molluscs in the seas. I'm the flattened-out old beer can. I'm the shopping trolley in the canal. I'm the note on the stave, the bird on the line. I'm the stave. I'm the line. I'm spiders. I'm seeds. I'm water. I'm heat. I'm the cotton of the sheet. I'm the tube that's in your side. I'm your urine in the tube. I'm your side. I'm your other side. I'm your other. I'm the coughing through the wall. I'm the cough. I'm the wall. I'm mucus. I'm the bronchial tubes. I'm inside. I'm

outside. I'm traffic. I'm pollution. I'm a fall of
horseshit on a country road a hundred years ago.
I'm the surface of that road. I'm what's below. I'm
what's above. I'm the fly. I'm the descendant of the
fly. I'm the descendant of the descendant of the
descendant of the descendant of the descendant of
the descendant of the fly. I'm the circle. I'm the
square. I'm all the shapes. I'm geometry. I haven't
even started with the telling you what I am. I'm
everything that makes everything. I'm everything
that unmakes everything. I'm fire. I'm flood. I'm
pestilence. I'm the ink, the paper, the grass, the
tree, the leaves, the leaf, the greenness in the leaf.
I'm the vein in the leaf. I'm the voice that tells no
story.

(Snorts.) There's no such thing.

Begging your pardon. There is. It's me.

Leaf, did you say?

I did say leaf, yes.

You? the leaf?

Are you deaf? I'm the leaf.

Just one lone single leaf, are you?

No. To be more exact. As I've already said. As
I've already made clear. I'm all the leaves.

You're all the leaves.

Yes.

So, have you fallen? Are you still waiting to fall?
In the autumn? In the summer if it's stormy?

Well, by definition –

And by *all the leaves* you mean, you're last year's leaves?

I –

And next year's leaves?

Yes, I –

You're all the old long-gone leaves of all the years? And all the leaves to come?

Yes, yes. Obviously. Christ almighty. I'm the leaves. I'm all the leaves. Okay?

And the falling thing? Yes or no?

Of course. It's what leaves do.

Then you can't trick me, whoever you are. You don't fool me for a minute.

(Silence.)

There's always, there'll always be, more story. That's what story is.

(Silence.)

It's the never-ending leaf-fall.

(Silence.)

Isn't it? Aren't you?

(Silence.)

Now that the actual autumn isn't far off, it's better weather. Up to now it has been fly-fetid, heavy-clouded, cool and autumnal all summer, pretty much since the first time Elisabeth went to the Post Office to do the Check & Send thing with her passport form.

It's now that her new passport arrives in the post.

Her hair must have passed the test after all. The placing of her eyes must also have passed the test.

She shows the new passport to her mother. Her mother points to the words European Union at the top of the cover of the passport and makes a sad face. Then she flicks through it.

What are all these drawings? she says. This passport has been illustrated like a Ladybird book.

A Ladybird book on acid, Elisabeth says.

I don't want a new passport if it's going to look

195

like this, her mother says. And all these men, all through it. Where are all the women? Oh, here's one. Is that Gracie Fields? Architecture? But who on earth? and is that *it*? Is this woman wearing the funny hat the only woman in the whole thing? Oh no. Here's another one, but sort of folded-in at the centre of a page, like an afterthought. And here's another couple, on the same page as the Scottish pipers, both ethnic stereotype dancers. Performing arts. Well, that's Scotland and women *and* a brace of continents all well and truly in their place.

She hands it back to Elisabeth.

If I'd seen this ridiculous thing that passes for a passport before the referendum, she says, I'd have known to be ready well ahead of time for what was so clearly on its way.

Elisabeth tucks the new passport beside the mirror in the bedroom her mother's made for her at the back of the house. Then she pulls on her coat to go to the bus stop.

Don't forget, her mother shouts through. Supper. I need you here by six. Zoe's coming.

Zoe is the person who was a BBC child actor when her mother was small, whom her mother met filming the episode of The Golden Gavel two weeks ago and with whom her mother is now firm friends. Zoe has been invited over to watch the opening of the Scottish Parliament, which her mother saved on her TV box at the start of the month and has already insisted on showing to Elisabeth. Her mother, who'd seen it several times already herself, was in tears from the start, from when the man doing the voiceover mentioned the words carved on the mace.

Wisdom. Justice. Compassion. Integrity.

It's the word integrity, her mother said. It does it every time. I hear it and I see in my head the faces of the liars.

Elisabeth grimaced. Every morning she wakes up feeling cheated of something. The next thing she thinks about, when she does, is the number of people waking up feeling cheated of something all over the country, no matter what they voted.

Uh huh, she said.

I'm still looking at properties up there, her mother said. I'm not leaving the EU.

It is all right for her mother. Her mother has had her life.

Rule Britannia, a bunch of thugs had been sing-shouting in the street at the weekend past Elisabeth's flat. Britannia rules the waves. First we'll get the Poles. And then we'll get the Muslims. Then we'll get the gyppos, then the gays. *You lot are on the run and we're coming after you*, a right-wing spokesman had shouted at a female MP on a panel on Radio 4 earlier that same Saturday. The chair of the panel didn't berate, or comment on, or even acknowledge the threat the man had just made.

Instead, he gave the last word to the Tory MP on the panel, who used what was the final thirty seconds of the programme to talk about the *real and disturbing cause for concern* – not the blatant threat just made on the air by one person to another – of *immigration*. Elisabeth had been listening to the programme in the bath. She'd switched the radio off after it and wondered if she'd be able to listen to Radio 4 in any innocence ever again. Her ears had undergone a sea-change. Or the world had.

But doth suffer a sea-change
Into something rich and –
Rich and what? she thought.
Rich and poor.

She rubbed the condensation off the mirror, stood in the echo of herself just standing in a bathroom. She looked at her blurred reflection.

Hi, Elisabeth had said down the phone to her mother next morning. It's me. At least, I think it is.

I know exactly what you mean, her mother said.

Can I come and stay at yours for a bit? I want to get some work done and to be a bit closer to, uh, home.

Her mother laughed and told her she could have the back room for as long as she needed.

Meanwhile Zoe, the 1960s child star, was also coming, to have Scotland played to her.

Zoe and I bonded over a silver sovereign holder,

her mother'd told her. I don't know if you know what they are, do you? They look like little fob-watches when they're closed, I've seen one or two on the TV antiques markets. There was one on top of a cabinet and Zoe picked it up and opened it and said oh what a pity, someone's taken all the clockwork out of it. And I said no, it's probably a sovereign holder. And she said blimey, is that the size of sovereignty? Old money, after all? Might have known. The original £1 coin. Soon to be worth 60p. We both laughed so loud we spoiled a take in the next room.

I want you to meet her, her mother says again now. She's cheered me up no end.

I won't forget, Elisabeth says.

She forgets as soon as she's through the door.

Time and time again. Even in the increased sleep period, with his head on a pillow and his eyes closed, hardly here, he does it, what he's always been able to do.

Endlessly charming, Daniel. Charmed life. How does he do it?

She'd brought the chair from the corridor. She'd shut the door to the room. She'd opened the book she bought today. She'd started to read, from the beginning, quite quietly, out loud. *It was the best of times, it was the worst of times, it was the age of wisdom, it was the age of foolishness, it was the epoch of belief, it was the epoch of incredulity, it was the season of Light, it was the season of Darkness, it was the spring of hope, it was the winter of despair, we had everything before us, we had nothing before us.* The words had acted like a charm. They'd released it all, in seconds. They'd made everything happening stand just far enough away.

It was nothing less than magic.

Who needs a passport?

Who am I? Where am I? What am I?

I'm reading.

Daniel lies there asleep like a person in a fairytale. She holds the opened book at its beginning in her hands. She says nothing at all out loud.

There was a time, she says inside her head, when I was very small and my mother banned me from seeing you, and I did what she'd asked but only for three days. By the morning of the third day I knew for the first time that one day I would die. So I blatantly ignored her. I went against her instructions. There was nothing she could do about it. It was only three days, and I prided myself on your not noticing or knowing about it at the time.

But I want to apologize for not being here these last years. It's ten years, all in. I'm really sorry. There wasn't anything I could do about it. I was hopelessly hurt, about something stupid.

Of course, it's possible that you didn't notice that absence either.

Myself, I thought about you the whole time. Even when I wasn't thinking about you, I thought about you.

Silence from Elisabeth, except for the sound of her breathing.

Silence from Daniel, except for the sound of his.

Not long after this, she falls asleep on the upright chair with her head leaning against the wall. She sits in the whited-out place in her dream.

The whited-out place this time is her flat.

To be truthful, it isn't *her* flat and she knows this in the dream; she's got used to the idea now that she'll probably never be able to buy a house. It's no big deal, no one can these days except people who're loaded, or whose parents die, or whose parents are loaded. But never mind. She has a lease. She has a lease on a white-walled flat in a dream. She can hear the people next door's TV through the wall. It is one of the ways you know you've got neighbours.

Someone knocks at the door. It'll be Daniel.

But it isn't. It's a girl. She has a face as blank as a piece of paper, blank as a blank screen. Elisabeth begins to panic. A blank screen means the computer is failing and all the knowledge is disappearing. There'll be no way she'll be able to access her workfiles. There'll be no way of knowing what's going on in the world right now. There'll be no way of getting in contact with anyone. There'll be no way she'll be able to do anything ever again.

The girl ignores Elisabeth. She sits down in the doorway so that Elisabeth can't shut the door. She gets out a book. She must be Miranda, from The

Tempest. Miranda from The Tempest is reading
Brave New World.

She looks up from her book as if she's just
realized Elisabeth is there too.

I've come to bring you news of our father,
she says.

Earlier today their father, according to the blank-
faced girl, had gone to buy a new laptop.

A present for you, the girl (Elisabeth's sister) says.
But then this happened.

Then Elisabeth sees, like she's watching a film,
what happened next.

On the way to John Lewis a man (her father?)
stops at the window of Cash Converters to look in
and see if anything there is cheaper. A woman stops
and looks in the window too. Are you looking at
the laptops? she says. Yes, Elisabeth's father says.
The thing is, the woman says, I'm about to go into
that shop and sell them my new laptop, and as I say,
it's brand new. I've got a new job in America and
I now don't need this new laptop. But if you're
looking to buy a laptop, I can sell it to you instead
of to Cash Converters and at a very good price for a
brand new laptop.

Elisabeth's father goes with the woman to a car
park where she opens the boot of a car and unzips a
holdall in the boot. She takes out a brand new
laptop. Elisabeth, in the dream, can smell how
new it is.

£600 cash, the woman says, does that sound fair? Yes, Elisabeth's father says. That sounds very fair. I'll go and get the money from a cash machine.

I'll come with you, the woman says putting the laptop back into the holdall and shutting the boot.

They go to a cash machine. He gets the money out. They go back to the car. He gives the woman the money. The woman opens the boot, takes the holdall out and hands it to him. She shuts the boot of the car and she drives away.

Then our father opened the bag, the girl with the blank face says. And there was nothing in that bag but onions. Onions and potatoes. Here.

She hands Elisabeth a holdall. Elisabeth opens it. It's full of potatoes and onions.

Thank you, Elisabeth says. Thank him for me.

She looks over to where the cooker should be. But there's nothing at all in the white-painted room.

Never mind, she thinks. When Daniel comes, he'll know a way of making something with these.

That's where she wakes up.

She remembers the dream for a fraction of a second, then she remembers where she is and she forgets the dream.

She stretches on the chair, her arms and shoulders, her legs.

So this is what sleeping with Daniel is like.

She smiles to herself.

(She's often wondered.)

**It was a standard sort of Wednesday in April in
1996.** Elisabeth was eleven. She was wearing new
rollerblades. When you put your weight on them
coloured lights lit up and flashed at the heels. You
couldn't see this yourself unless it was dark outside
and you put all the lights out in your bedroom or
drew the blind and pressed down on them with
your hands.

Daniel was at the front gate.

I'm going to the theatre, he said. The outdoor
theatre. Want to come too?

He told her it was a play about civilization,
colonization and imperialism.

It sounds a bit boring, she said.

Trust me, Daniel said.

So she went, and it wasn't boring, it was really
good, about a father and a daughter. It was also

about fairness and unfairness, and people getting hypnotized on an island and hatching plots against each other to see who could take control of the island, and some characters were meant to be the slaves and other characters got to be freed. But mostly it was about a girl whose father, a magician, was sorting out her future for her. In the end the daughter could have been in it a bit more than she was, but all the same it was still really good; in the end Elisabeth was nearly crying when the grown-old father stepped forward without his magic cloak and stick and asked the people in the audience to clap because if they didn't he'd be trapped forever in the play on the fake island with its cardboard scenery. If they hadn't, it was really very much as if he *might* still be stuck there in the open air theatre standing in the dark all night.

It was also quite exciting to be able, just by clapping your hands, to free someone from something.

She rollerbladed home in front of Daniel so Daniel would be able to see the lights light up.

When she was in bed that night she remembered her feet and the pavement passing so fast beneath them and thought how strange it was that she could remember totally useless details about things like cracks in a pavement more clearly than she could recall anything about her own father.

The next day at breakfast she said to her mother,

I couldn't sleep last night.

Oh dear, her mother said. Well, you'll sleep tonight instead.

I couldn't sleep for a reason, Elisabeth said.

Uh huh? her mother said.

Her mother was reading the paper.

I couldn't sleep, Elisabeth said, because I realized I can't remember a single thing about what my father's face looks like.

Well, you're lucky, her mother said from behind the paper.

She turned the page, folded it against another page, shook the paper into shape again and put it back up in the air between them.

Elisabeth strapped her rollerblades on, laced them up and went round to Daniel's house. Daniel was in the back garden. Elisabeth rollerbladed down the path.

Oh hello, Daniel said. It's you. What you reading?

I couldn't get to sleep last night, she said.

Wait, Daniel said. First of all, tell me. What are you reading?

Clockwork, she said. It's really good. I told you about it yesterday. The one about people making up the story but then the story becomes true and starts to happen and is really terrible.

I remember, Daniel said. They stop the bad thing happening by singing a song.

Yes, Elisabeth said.

If only life were so simple, Daniel said.

That's what I'm saying, Elisabeth said. I couldn't sleep.

Because of the book? Daniel said.

Elisabeth told him about the pavement, her feet, her father's face. Daniel looked grave. He sat down on the lawn. He patted the place on the grass next to him.

It's all right to forget, you know, he said. It's good to. In fact, we have to forget things sometimes. Forgetting it is important. We do it on purpose. It means we get a bit of a rest. Are you listening? We have to forget. Or we'd never sleep ever again.

Elisabeth was crying now like a much younger child cries. Crying came out of her like weather.

Daniel put his hand flat against her back.

What I do when it distresses me that there's something I can't remember, is. Are you listening?

Yes, Elisabeth said through the crying.

I imagine that whatever it is I've forgotten is folded close to me, like a sleeping bird.

What kind of bird? Elisabeth said.

A wild bird, Daniel said. Any kind. You'll know what kind when it happens. Then, what I do is, I just hold it there, without holding it too tight, and I let it sleep. And that's that.

Then he asked her if it was true that the

rollerskates with the lights on the backs of them only worked on roads, and if it was true that the lights in the backs of them didn't come on at all if you rollerskated on grass.

Elisabeth stopped crying.

They're called rollerblades, she said.

Rollerblades, Daniel said. Right. Well?

And you can't rollerblade on grass, she said.

Can't you? Daniel said. How very disappointing truth is sometimes. Can't we try?

There'd be no point, she said.

Can't we try anyway? he said. We might disprove the general consensus.

Okay, Elisabeth said.

She got up. She wiped her face on her sleeve.

Recalled to life, Elisabeth says. Hunger, want and nothing. The whole city's in a storm at sea and that's just the beginning. Savagery's coming. Heads are going to roll.

Elisabeth is in the hall hanging her coat up. Her mother has just introduced her to her new friend Zoe and asked Elisabeth how far through A Tale of Two Cities they are today.

Who's Mr Gluck? her mother's new friend Zoe says.

Mr Gluck is a jolly old gay man who used to be our neighbour years back, her mother says. She was very fond of him, he befriended her as a child. She was a difficult child. Pity me. A very difficult child to read.

No he isn't. Yes I was and still am. And no I wasn't. In that order, Elisabeth says.

See? her mother says.

I like a difficult read myself, Zoe says.

She smiles at Elisabeth with genuine friendliness. She is in her sixties maybe. She is handsome and unfussily stylish. She is now apparently a pretty well-known psychoanalyst. (Elisabeth had laughed when her mother told her this, at last you're seeing someone after all the years you've needed to, she'd said.) She bears a fleeting ghost of a resemblance to that girl dancing with the phonebox in the film back then; the girl-ghost is a technicolor shimmer somewhere still about her person. Her older self is warm, bright like an apple still high up in a tree after all the others have been picked. Meanwhile Elisabeth's mother is making an effort, wearing make-up and a set of brand new looking linen clothes like the ones they sell in the expensive shop in the village.

And you've kept in touch all these years, Zoe says.

We'd lost touch, actually, her mother says, till a neighbour tracked me down on the net and let me know he'd packed up his house, sold his old Barbara Hepworth piece of holy stone –

Maquette, Elisabeth says.

Oh my goodness, Zoe says. He's got taste.

– and signed himself into a care home, her mother says. And I happened to tell Elisabeth, who'd been out here to see me a total of, I kid you not, once, in a total of, I kid you not, six years, I told her on the phone, I said oh by the way, old

214

Mr Gluck. He's in this place called The Maltings apparently not far from here. And I kid you not. She's been here every week, all this summer. Twice, sometimes. And now she's living here for a while. Nice having a daughter again. So far, anyway.

Thanks, Elisabeth says.

And now I'm looking forward to a bit of fine-tuned attention myself in my later years, her mother says. All those books I've never read, Middlemarch, Moby-Dick, War and Peace. Not that I'll be able to do my later years quite like Mr Gluck has. He's a hundred and ten by now.

He's a what? Zoe says.

She always gets his age completely wrong. He's only a hundred and one, Elisabeth says.

Zoe shakes her head.

Only, she says. Blimey. Seventy five'll do. Anything after that, bonus. Well. I'm saying that now. Who knows what I'll say if I get to seventy five?

He used to set up a projector and a screen in his back garden on summer nights, her mother says, and show her old films, I'd look out the window, it'd be a starry night and they'd be sitting in a little box of light. That was back in the years when we still had summers. When we still had seasons, not just the monoseason we have now. And do you remember the time he threw his watch into the river –

Canal, Elisabeth says.

– and told you it was a time and motion study? her mother says.

What a fine friendship, Zoe says. And you go and see him every week? And read to him?

I love him, Elisabeth says.

Zoe nods.

Her mother rolls her eyes.

He's pretty much comatose, she says in a more hushed voice. I'm afraid. He won't.

He isn't comatose, Elisabeth says.

When she says it she feels the edge of anger on her own voice. She calms her voice down and speaks again.

He's just sleeping, she says, but for very long times. He's not comatose. He's resting. It'll have tired him out, packing up his house, all his things.

She sees her mother shake her head at her new friend.

Me, I'll be throwing it all away, Zoe says. Canal, river, wherever's nearest. Or giving it away. No point keeping any of it.

Elisabeth goes through to the sunroom and lies flat out on the sofa. She'd forgotten the film nights, Chaplin getting a job at the circus as an assistant then pressing by mistake the button he's been told not to press on the magician's table and the ducks and the doves and the piglets coming flying out of all the hidden compartments.

So I stood in the hall and phoned the number

every week, I was desperate, her mother is saying through in the kitchen, 01 811 8055, I still remember it off by heart, it meant I hardly ever saw the programme, I was always in the hall. But once I'd had the idea, I thought it was so funny, I thought I was the height of wit. So, every week. Then one week I actually got through. And the switchboard girl, they used to sit at the back of the studio and take the calls and write the swaps down, she came on the phone and she said the magic words Multi-Coloured Swap Shop, and I said it, I'm Wendy Parfitt and I'd like to swap my kingdom for a horse, and they put it up on the screen and showed it as one of their top ten swaps, Wendy Parfitt, OFFERS kingdom, WANTS horse.

I once met him, Noel, her friend says. Well, thirty seconds. Very exciting. In the staff canteen.

Our whole life, her mother is saying. My whole life, as a child. The night after our father's funeral, our mother – I suppose she didn't know what else to do – switching on the TV, and we all sat there, her too, watching The Waltons, as if it'd make things better, make everything be normal again.

All as mysterious to me, all as exciting, as comforting, as it was to you, her mother's friend is saying. Even though I was meant to be being such a part of it. And now all anyone wants to know is whether there was any abuse. Did anyone ever do anything they shouldn't have to us. The people who ask, they're *longing* to ask, not just that, they're longing to hear something bad, they want it to have gone wrong, they always seem disappointed when I say no, when I say that it was a great time, that I loved working, I loved above all being a working actress, I loved it too that I got given the most fantastic clothes, that I taught myself to smoke in the back of the car that picked me up for work and took me home from work – and if I say *that*, the thing about cigarettes, the eyebrows go up and it's like *that*'s an abuse of innocence, the urge I had to be my older self. The urge we all have to be older, to not be the child any more.

Elisabeth wakes up. She sits up.

It's getting dark outside.

She looks at her phone. It's near nine.

She can hear the low murmur of conversation across the hall. They've moved to the sitting room. They must have had supper without her.

They're talking about a particular room they went into in one of the shops on the Golden Gavel shoot. Her mother has told her about this room. It was huge, the room, her mother told her, with nothing in it but thousands of old sherry glasses piled inside each other.

Like entering what you think is going to be history and finding endless sad fragility, Zoe says. One kick. Disaster. Careful where you tread. And all the old dial-phones.

218

The ceramic dogs, her mother says.

The inkwells. (Zoe.)

The engraved silver matchboxes, Anchor and Lion hallmark, Birmingham, turn of the century. (Her mother.)

You're pretty good at that stuff. (Zoe.)

I watch a lot of TV. (Her mother.)

Got to get out more. (Zoe.)

The butter churn. (Her mother.) The wall-mounted coffee grinder. (Zoe.) The Poole pottery. The Clarice Cliff fakes. The tinplate Japanese robots. (Elisabeth can no longer tell now whose voice is whose.) The Pelham Puppets, remember them, still in their boxes. The clocks. The war medals. The engraved crystal. The nests of tables. The tiles. The decanters. The cabinets. The apprentice pieces. The plant-stands. The old books of photographs. The sheet music. The paintings. And paintings. And paintings.

All across the country all the things from the past stacked on the shelves in the shops and the barns and the warehouses, piled into display units and on top of display units, spilling up stairs from the cellars of the shops, down stairs from the attic rooms of the shops, like a huge national orchestra biding its time, the bows held just above the strings, all the fabrics muted, all the objects holding still and silent till the shops empty of people, till the alarms play their electronic beeps at the doors, till the keys turn in the locks in the thousands of shops and barns and warehouses all across the country.

Then, when darkness falls, the symphony. Oh. Oh, that's a beautiful idea. The symphony of the sold and the discarded. The symphony of all the lives that had these things in them once. The symphony of worth and worthlessness. The Clarice Cliff fakes would be flutey. The brown furniture would be bass, low. The photographs in the old damp-stained albums would be whispery through their tracing paper. The silver would be pure. The wickerwork would be reedy. The porcelains? They'd have voices that sound like they might break any minute. The wood things would be tenor. Yes, but would the real things sound any different from the reproduction things?

The women start to laugh.

Elisabeth can smell smoke.

No. She can smell dope.

She lies back down on the sofa and listens to them laughing about the number of times they spoiled the set-up of shots on their filming of The Golden Gavel by laughing in the wrong places or not saying the right thing. She gathers, from what they say, that there was quite a fuss caused by her mother's stubbornness, refusing to say the hello to the person who owned the antiques shop they were filming in as if they were just meeting for the first time, when truthfully they'd met an hour beforehand and she'd done the take already five times. *Hello again!* she said every time. *Cut!* the production team yelled.

I just couldn't do it, her mother says. It was so stupidly false. I was hopeless.

You were. And it gave me such hope, the new friend says.

Elisabeth smiles. That's nice.

She sits up. She goes through to the kitchen. The supper things are all still out on the table waiting to be cooked.

She goes through to the sitting room instead and the room is fuggy with dope. Her mother's new friend Zoe is sitting on the chaise longue and her mother is sitting in her new friend's lap. They've got their arms round each other like the famous Rodin statue, in the middle of the kiss.

Ah, Elisabeth says.

Zoe opens her eyes.

Uh-oh. Caught, she says.

Elisabeth watches her mother struggle to retain not just her composure but any balance at all on her new friend's knee.

She winks at her mother's new friend through the dope smoke.

She's been waiting for you since she was ten years old, Elisabeth says. I'll make supper, shall I?

It was a sunny Friday evening more than a decade ago, in the spring of 2004. Elisabeth was nearly twenty. She was staying in. She was watching Alfie, a film meant to have an appearance by Pauline Boty in it. The film starred Michael Caine as a philanderer. It had been a very groundbreaking film at the time because Caine as Alfie spoke so frankly, straight to camera, and about sexual adventuring.

Quite early on in the film Michael Caine walks along a bright sunny 1960s London street and knocks on the glass of a window saying Prompt Service Within, to get the attention of a young woman in the window.

It's her.

She turns, looks delighted and beckons him in. As he goes through the door he switches the open sign to closed and follows her to the back. Then he takes her in his arms and kisses her, and then slips behind the clothes-rack for a comedy quick one three seconds long with her.

It was definitely Pauline Boty.

It was filmed the year before she died.

Her name wasn't in the credits.

I was having a beautiful little life, and I couldn't see it, the Michael Caine voiceover said. *There was this manageress of a dry-cleaner's.* He went into the shop, behind the clothes with the girl, then a few moments later came out the other side saying, *and I was getting a suit cleaned in the bargain.*

According to what Elisabeth had read about her life, Boty was already pregnant in these shots.

She was wearing a bright blue top. Her hair was the colour of corn.

But you can't write that in a dissertation. You can't write, *she made it look like a blast.* You can't write, *she looked like she'd be really good fun, like she was full of energy,* or *energy comes off her in waves.* You can't write, even though it's a lot more like the language expected, *though she's in that film for less than twenty seconds she adds something crucial and crucially female about pleasure to its critique of the contemporary new and liberated ethos, which was indeed what she was also doing with her aesthetic.*

Blah.

Elisabeth opened the Boty catalogue again and

flicked through it. The wild bright colours came off the pages at her as she did.

She stopped on one of the long-lost pictures, the one of Christine Keeler on the chair. Keeler had slept with two men, one had been Secretary of State for War in the government in London, one had been a Russian diplomat, and it was about blatant lying in Parliament, then about who had most power and who owned information about nuclear weapons – except that it soon, ostensibly at least, became about something else altogether, about who owned Keeler, who farmed her out, and who did or didn't make money out of it.

The Boty picture, Scandal 63, had been missing since the year it was painted. There were only photographs of it. In the finished version, Boty had painted Keeler on her Danish chair surrounded by abstracts, though some of the abstracts looked more figurative: that, there on the left, arguably, was a tragedy mask; that down there was a woman having what looked like an orgasm. Above Keeler on the chair, on something resembling a dark balcony, Boty had painted, a bit like decapitated heads on a city wall, the heads and shoulders of four men, two black men and two white men. In an earlier version, which you could see half of in a picture with Boty herself in it, you got a sense of the size of the picture, big enough to come up quite far past Boty's waist. In this earlier version Boty didn't use the famous image of Keeler in the chair. She changed her mind for the later version, and did.

Elisabeth wrote in pencil on a page of her foolscap pad: *art like this examines and makes possible a reassessment of the outer appearances of things by transforming them into something other than themselves. An __image of an image__ means the image can be seen with new objectivity, with liberation from the original.*

Dissertation blah.

She looked at the photograph of Boty standing beside Scandal 63. She took the book over to the window to see the photographs in what was left of the daylight.

No one knew who'd commissioned this painting.

No one knew where it was now, if it was still anywhere, if it still existed.

She looked again at how the mask, the gargoyle tragedy face, formed and unformed itself at the side of the picture.

Elisabeth had tried to read up about the Scandal scandal so she could think about and write about this picture. She'd read everything she could find online and everything in the library: some cultural books about the 1960s, a couple of books by Keeler, a copy of the Denning Report on the Scandal scandal. She hadn't known that proximity to lies, even just reading about them, could make you feel so ill. The whole thing was a bit like being made to watch something as innocent as Alfie through a gimp mask and a lot of painful S&M gear you'd never agreed to wear in the first place.

In her head whenever she thought of the true-life story round the Scandal scandal, one tiny detail in the story barbed into her like a fishhook.

An art historian called Blunt, who'd soon have his own sex/intelligence scandal to deal with, had turned up, in the middle of the Scandal trial in 1963, at an art gallery in London where there was an exhibition of portraiture. It was the work of Stephen Ward, who'd become the villain or the fall guy of the scandal at the time and who'd shortly be dead in what looked to be suicide. Ward had done portraits of rich and famous people of the time, aristocracy, royalty, political royalty, and many of them were on show here. Blunt had handed over a massive amount of cash and bought them all, everything in the gallery, outright.

He'd apparently taken them away and, the books and articles said, had them destroyed.

How had he destroyed them? Had he set them alight in some well-to-do hearth? Had he doused them in petrol in an isolated country house garden?

What Elisabeth imagined was that there was a hole dug deep in a stubbly harvested cornfield somewhere in the middle of nowhere by a tractor-sized digger, properly deep, deep enough for a couple of bodies. A small team of people stood

227

round the rim of the hole and tossed into it portrait after portrait, making a mass grave of portraits, a pile-up of VIPs.

Then she imagined the small team of people dragging and shoving a freshly slaughtered horse or cow off the back of a lorry into the digger's mouth. She imagined the digger mechanically positioning the horse or cow carcass above the hole with the portraits in it, then the driver pushing the lever and the carcass dropping into the hole. She imagined the digger shunting the field's earth over the art and the carcass and filling the hole. She imagined the treads of the digger flattening the mound, and the people dusting their clothes down, washing the earth off their hands and cleaning it out of their nails when they got back to somewhere with water.

The horse or the cow was an extra flourish. If Elisabeth were a painter it'd be how she'd have signified the rot.

Sometimes she imagined the Boty Scandal 63 painting in there too, the carcass falling on to it, the weight of it splitting the picture's wooden stretcher. She imagined Blunt coming up the stairs of the house Boty's studio was in, his pockets full of banknotes, him not deigning to touch the banister with the filth of the pre-war years, the war years and the post-war decade still deep in its wooden ridges.

But you can't write any of that in a dissertation.

Look, she'd been doodling in the margin. There were swirls and waves and spirals.

She looked back at what she'd actually written down. *Art like this examines and makes possible a reassessment of the outer appearances of things.*

She laughed.

She took her pencil, rubbed out the capital A with the rubber on its tip, made it the lower case word *art,* then added a completely new word right at the front of the sentence so the sentence began

Arty art

Portrait in words of our next door neighbour

Our Next door neighbour to our new house we have moved to is the most elegant neighbour I have so far had. He is not old. My mother will not let me ask him the questions about being a neighbour that I am meant to be asking him for the portrait in words project we are meat to do. She says I am not allowed to bother him. She has said that she will buy us a new video player and the Beauty and The Beast video if I make up I am asking him the questions in stead of ask them in real life. To be honest I would rather not have the video or video player I would rather ask him them, what it is like to have new neighbuors and is it the same for him. Here are the questions I would ask him 1 what is it like to have neighbours 2 what is it like to be a neighbour 3 what it is like to be meant to be old but not to be 4 why his house is full of pictures why they are not like the pictures we have in our house and lastly 5 why there is music playing when ever you walk close to the front door of our next door neighbour.

Next morning in 2016, the little TV up on the shelf in the kitchen is on but with the sound turned down; it must have been on, lighting and darking the kitchen by itself, all night.

Elisabeth is the only person up so far. She fills the coffeepot with water and puts it on the ring and as she turns the cooker on she sees on the screen two young twenty-somethings shopping separately in a supermarket advert suddenly simultaneously dropping the products in their hands, a loaf of bread, a couple of packets of pasta, and finding themselves in each other's arms as if by magic, then waltzing in amazement that they know how to waltz. In the next aisle a small child catches the carton of eggs his parents have just let slip. He watches his parents as they spin round and round together by a pyramid of cheeses. Near the fish counter an old couple, the man

233

holding a tin of something up to his glasses, the woman holding on to the trolley like a zimmer, both look upwards, like they hear something above them. They exchange a knowing look. Then the woman holding the trolley pushes it away, steps backwards unbelievably light and poised on her feet, the man lets his stick fall to the ground, bows low to her and they start waltzing with old-style grace.

Elisabeth runs across to the shelf for the remote but she only gets the sound back on for the final seconds of the ad, where the child who caught the eggs shrugs his shoulders at the camera, the last shot is the sunlit summer supermarket from outside, people dancing in its car park, the warm middle-aged male voiceover saying: *all year round making a song and a dance about you.*

When her mother gets up she finds Elisabeth watching an advert for a supermarket over and over again on the laptop.

What's that burning smell? she says.

She opens the windows, cleans up round the cooker and throws away the singed dishtowel.

It begins with a supermarket car park full of cars heaped with snow, snow falling. Then the song and the dance. Then, as the song ends, the summer supermarket from outside.

Pretty gloomy song for supermarket advertising, her mother says. Then again I can't listen to anything these days without feeling maudlin.

Oh, I don't know, Elisabeth says. You've always been maudlin.

True enough. Over the years I've had a substantial career in maudlin, her mother says taking the computer.

Has her mother been this witty all these years and Elisabeth just hasn't realized?

Mike Ray and the Milky Ways, her mother says.

Never heard of them, Elisabeth says.

Her mother looks it up.

One-hit wonders, 1962, Summer Brother Autumn Sister (Gluck/Klein). Number 19, September 1962, her mother says. Well well. Maybe you're right. Maybe our Mr Gluck did write it after all.

Verse 1:

Snow is falling in the summer / Leaves are falling in the spring / Gone the reasons, gone the seasons / Time has gone and taken everything
    Chorus: Summer brother autumn sister / Keeping time through time / Autumn mellow autumn yellow / Give me back a reason to rhyme

Verse 2:

I will find her in the autumn / Autumn kissed her. Autumn mist / Summer brother autumn sister / Autumn's gone so summers don't exist

Chorus x 1
Bridge:

Summer brother autumn sister / Time and time again
are gone / Out of season I will find her / With time's
fallen leaves behind her / Every time I sing this song

Chorus x 2 Ad lib to fade

(© words & music Gluck/Klein)

There is almost nothing else online about *Gluck
songwriter,* or *Gluck lyricist* or *Gluck/Klein
words & music* except links back to this song and
to the supermarket advert. There are lots of those
links. Twenty five thousand, seven hundred and five
people have watched the advert on YouTube.

Were you just playing the Milky Ways? Zoe says
coming through to the living room in Elisabeth's
mother's bathrobe. What's that burning smell?

She goes through to the kitchen whistling the
chorus.

Elisabeth checks for the song on the online
charts. It's doing rather well. She search-engines the
contact details for the supermarket's head office.

What's your second name? she says to Zoe.

Spencer-Barnes, Zoe says. Why?

Elisabeth calls a number on her phone.

Hello, she says. This is Elisabeth Demand, I'm
calling from the Spencer-Barnes Agency, can you

put me through to your marketing department? No, that's fine, answerphone is fine. Thank you.

(Pause.) Hello, I'm calling from the Spencer-Barnes Agency, my name is Elisabeth Demand, that's D, e, m, a, n and d, and I'm calling on behalf of my client Mr Daniel Gluck whose copyright via your use in your current campaign of Mr Gluck's 1962 hit song Summer Brother Autumn Sister is being infringed every time your latest television commercial is aired. Obviously if you or your agency partners will be so good as to contact me, which you can do on this number – clearly we'd appreciate your alacrity – and negotiate and then be ready to transfer immediately funds totalling what we agree is legally owed to our client Mr Gluck, then the matter will cease to be problematic for us as far as both our client and the question of infringement law is concerned. I'll wait to hear from you that the situation has been resolved. If I haven't heard within twenty four hours we'll be taking action, and I'd suggest at least blanket suspension of your commercial until this has been taken in hand. Many thanks.

She left her number at the end of the message.

Infringement, her mother says. Alacrity. Via.

Elisabeth shrugs.

Do you think it'll work? her mother says.

Worth a try, Elisabeth says. I bet they think he's long gone.

What about the other people? Zoe says. What about Mike Ray? The Milky Ways?

My only concern is Daniel, Elisabeth says. I mean Mr Gluck.

Your girl's a powerhouse, Zoe says.

Isn't she. But never underestimate the source, her mother says.

The source? Elisabeth says.

Me, her mother says.

That'll be the day, Elisabeth says.

Yet another good old song, Zoe says.

She starts singing it.

It is like magic has happened in my life, Elisabeth's mother whispers to Elisabeth when Zoe's left the room.

Unnatural, Elisabeth says.

Who'd have known, who'd have guessed, it'd be love, at this late stage, that'd see me through? Elisabeth's mother says.

Unhealthy, Elisabeth says. I forbid it. You're not to.

She gives her mother a hug and a kiss.

That's enough, her mother says.

What's this book? Zoe says.

She comes through from the hall.

Who's this artist? she says. These are wonderful.

She sits down at the kitchen table with the old Pauline Boty catalogue open at the painting called 5 4 3 2 1.

One of the people my erudite daughter educates people about, Elisabeth's mother says.

Artist from the 1960s, Elisabeth says. The only British female Pop artist.

Ah, Zoe says. I didn't know there were any.

There were, Elisabeth says.

Victim of abuse, I expect, Zoe says.

She winks at Elisabeth. Elisabeth laughs.

Just the usual humdrum contemporary misogynies, she says.

Committed suicide, Zoe says.

Nope, Elisabeth says.

Went mad, then, Zoe says.

Nope. Just the usual humdrum completely sane occasional depressions, Elisabeth says.

Ah. Died tragically, then, Zoe says.

Well, that's one reading of it, Elisabeth says. My own preferred reading is: free spirit arrives on earth equipped with the skill and the vision capable of blasting the tragic stuff that happens to us all into space, where it dissolves away to nothing whenever you pay any attention to the lifeforce in her pictures.

Oh, that's good, Zoe says. That's very good. All the same. I bet she was ignored.

She was after she died, Elisabeth says.

I bet it goes like this, Zoe says. Ignored. Lost. Rediscovered years later. Then ignored. Lost. Rediscovered again years later. Then ignored. Lost. Rediscovered ad infinitum. Am I right?

Elisabeth laughs out loud.

Have you actually *done* one of my daughter's courses? her mother says.

What's her story, then, this girl? Zoe says.

She's looking at the photograph of Boty young and laughing, not yet twenty, on the inside fold of the catalogue cover.

Her story? Elisabeth says. Got ten minutes?

Autumn. 1963. Scandal 63. Up till last night the most prominent Keeler was right here, centre canvas, shouldering her way into the upper balcony, poised at the midpoint of the upper echelon between Ward and Profumo – at least, one of the Christine images was. Till last night there'd been several Christine images at different points on the canvas. One Christine image was striding along, another was naked, smiling prettily at the foot of the frame, another was in ecstasy down below the feet of the central Christine walking above swinging her handbag. But then last night at the Establishment Lewis was there, he was at the bar.

Lewis took the press photo that had spread like Spanish flu. Iconic. He'd seen what Pauline was working on, he photographed it actually. He'd come to the studio and photographed her holding

Scandal 63 on one side, Ready Steady Go on the other, kind of equivalents, and he saw her come in and he said, want to come up and see my Keelers? and Pauline said I say, what can you possibly mean, I'm a married woman you know, yes please. So they'd gone upstairs to his place above the club and he showed her and Clive the shots under the magnifiers, and she'd looked up close at the original, *the* image. Keeler with her arms up, chin on both her fists, it was splendid.

Then she'd noticed along from it on the contact sheet the slightly different version of the same.

So she said to Lewis, can you maybe make me that one up, please?

It was a good one, looked less coy, more self-protecting. One arm was down. You could see what Keeler looks like when she's thinking.

I'll do Keeler thinking, she thought. Keeler the Thinker.

Then she pointed at the marks on Keeler's leg, quite visible the bruising in the magnification.

Gosh, she said.

Can't see it in the money shot, Lewis said. Papers, too grainy.

So now she was repainting the commission. It would be full of questions now, not statements. It would still look like the image everyone thought they knew, but at the same time *not be* it. Keeler trompe l'oeil. And even an eye that didn't at first

242

notice, even an eye that took the pose for granted, would still know, unconsciously – something not quite as you expect, as you remember, as it's meant to be, can't quite put your finger.

The image and the life: well, she was used to that. There was Pauline and there was the image – feather boa flung about, winking at the camera, it was fun. High in confidence. Low in confidence. Dressed as Marilyn in the college revues, *I wanna be loved by you*. Playing Doris Day, *every body loves my body*. Little-girl song in a grown-woman voice, *daddy wouldn't buy me a bauhaus, I've got a little cat* (gasps at how she made sure they knew cat meant cunt). *Diamonds are a girl's, my armpits are charmpits* (gasps at the word armpits, not a word ever heard out loud). At the Royal College, where girls were so rare they made you stare, where the architects hadn't bothered putting women's toilets in the blueprint, she walked the corridors hearing the whispers as she went by, *rumour is, that one there's actually read Proust*, she put her arm round the boy and said it's true darling *and* Genet *and* de Beauvoir *and* Rimbaud *and* Colette, I've read all the men and the women of French letters, oh and Gertrude Stein as well, don't you know about women and their tender buttons?

The bomb was going to drop. They'd maybe only a few years to live.

A boy asked her, *why do you wear so much*

bright red lipstick, all the better to kiss you with she said and jumped out of her chair and came after him, he ran away, he was actually sort of terrified, she chased him out of the college and across the grass and up the pavement till he leapt on the back of a passing bus and she stood holding herself, she was laughing so much. A man, quite an old one, a very nice one, had made her laugh like that too by crawling towards her on his hands and knees across the room kissing the floor between him and her as he did; he was the songwriter, came to the flat, she called him Gershwin for fun. He asked her, looking at her Belmondo with the hat, *who's he*? Film star, French, she said, that picture's all heart-throb versus cunt-throb don't you think? and poor old Gershwin blushed all the way to his tips – ears, toes, everywhere he had a tip blushing, sweet older chap he couldn't help it, he was from another time. Well, they almost all were. Even the people meant to be from *now* were really from *then*. He was in the studio the other day, looked at 5 4 3 2 1, *what does it say*? he'd said and he'd read it out loud. *Oh for a fu–. Oh. Ah. I see. How very, ah, Shakespearianly put.* Well, if you're Gershwin, she said, I'm the Wimbledon Bard-o. Get it? *Oh yes,* he said, *Bard, Bardot. How apt.*

He liked her a lot.

Oh well.

Couldn't be helped.

Imagine if pictures in a gallery weren't just pictures but were actually sort of alive.

Imagine if time could be kind of suspended, rather than us be suspended in it.

She had no idea sometimes, to be honest, what she was trying to do. To be vital, she supposed.

Low in confidence, only sixteen, when a tutor suggested to her *stained glass isn't just for churches, it can be for anywhere. It doesn't have to be for holy things, it can be for anything.* High in confidence leaving the little corner on The Only Blonde In The World just the bare canvas like a corner of the painting had come away by itself, trompe l'oeil like you could peel them off and know that's what they were, images. Marilyn all dazzling, hurrying by in Some Like It Hot, cutting through abstraction with her brightness. Could you paint the female orgasm? It *was* Marilyn. It was coloured circles, lovely, lovely, and everything was exciting, TV was exciting, radio was exciting, London was exciting, full of exciting people from all over the world, and theatre was exciting, an empty fairground was exciting, cigarette packets were exciting, milk bottle tops were exciting, Greece was exciting, Rome was exciting, a clever woman in a hostel's shower room wearing a man's shirt to sleep in was exciting, Paris – exciting (*I am alone in Paris!! wherever I go I am followed or asked to take coffee etc. etc. otherwise Paris is*

245

marvellous, the painting – no words possible).
High in confidence, art could be anything, beer
cans were a new kind of folk art, film stars a new
mythology, nostalgia of NOW. It was exciting
when she worked out the photographers taking the
photos of *her* couldn't cut her *art* out of their
pictures if she posed as *part* of her art.

(Wrong.

Blast.

They still managed to cut round her and slice the
art out and away, leaving the breast and the thigh
bits, of course.)

Get my paintbrushes into the shot, will
you, Mike?

She was wearing a hat, a shirt and her
underwear, mimicking as closely as she could Celia
in the portrait, except she'd taken her jeans off to
be sure they'd keep both her and the picture in the
picture. But Lewis and Michael were great boys,
she kind of liked them immensely. They let her tell
them how to set up the shots and mostly they did as
she asked. Happy to pose nude. I like nakedness. I
mean who doesn't, to be honest? I'm a person. I'm
an intelligent nakedness. An intellectual body. I'm a
bodily intelligence. Art's full of nudes and I'm a
thinking, choosing nude. I'm the artist as nude. I'm
the nude as artist.

A great many men don't understand a woman
full of joy, even more don't understand paintings

full of joy by a woman. It's really all based on sex the whole thing, look, the bananas and fountains and that huge mouth and the hand, well, they're all phallic symbols. *Well, anyway,* they say, *I'm a man, and being a man is lots better than being a woman.*

She saw the notice pinned to the side of the building, bright yellow, saying in different coloured letters CRAZY COTTAGE then underneath in blue the bigger letters BRIGITTE'S BIKINI then small in faded black COME IN & SEE then a little THE on the side then huge in red SEX KITTEN. Take my photo looking at this, please, Mike, she said. She came right up to the side of the building as if she were coming round its corner and simply sort of reading the sign because that's what she was, a girl reading the world.

But love was terribly important. She didn't mean romantic love. Generalized sort of love. Enjoying oneself was terribly important. Sex could be as varied as being alive could be varied. Passion always sounded to her like something without humour in it. A passionate moment for her –

I can remember once sitting opposite my brother and feeling so much love for him that it was almost as though I was knitted to him.

This lovely feeling (she'd say to the writer interviewing her for a book) lasted for, say, half an hour. But she'd married her husband because he *liked* women, he knew they weren't *things,* or something you didn't quite know about. He accepted me intellectually, which men find very difficult.

High in confidence. Low in confidence. Her mother was out in her father's English rose garden pruning the roses; her mother made the dresses and made the meals. Out in the Carshalton garden with the pruning shears her mother said it way before James Brown, *it's a man's world*, moving the mark on the sherry bottle so her father wouldn't notice, her mother, Veronica, banned back in the day from taking a place at the Slade by her own father, grieving for that place all her secateur life, working on Pauline's father to let her, Wimbledon Art School. It was her mother took her to America on the QE2, her mother listening to Maria Callas at full volume (when her father was out), shouting at the radio news (in the kitchen when her father wasn't in the kitchen), her mother who fell ill, Pauline was eleven, endless X-rays for everyone, scans, her mother who was going to die. The family went to chaos, it was good the chaos, except for the depressions. No, it was formative. Lost a lung, her mother, but she was kind of perfectly all right, she was keeping a scrapbook of the cuttings from the papers. PAULINE PAINTS POPS. And ALL MY OWN WORK. (That was the headline on Pauline hanging an abstract in the London Labour Party Trades Union Congress Headquarters.) *Actresses often have tiny brains. Painters often have huge beards. Imagine a brainy actress who is also a painter and also a blonde.*

Imagine.

Her father was stern. Her father disapproved. Her father had very strong reservations. Desirable? a semi? I daren't say anything or daddy will be upset. Half Belgian, half Persian, staunch British conservative, he'd seen the Himalayas and Harrogate and had chosen accountancy. His father'd been killed by pirates (true). His mother's family had been shipbuilders on the Euphrates. So the Norfolk Broads is where he kept his own boat, and the rules of cricket, the making of tea the way it should be made were what to measure life by.

He didn't even want me to work when I left school.

The fights were sort of huge, often before breakfast, the stupidest worst time to fight with him. Her older brothers flinched and shook their heads. Her brothers had it too, men had it too, maybe even worse – the brother who wanted to go to art school, their father made him an accountant. *She* got to go eventually, well, after all, not a proper job, so it was maybe more okay, for a girl, to.

But her brothers, when she was little. *Shut up, you're only a girl.* Used to want to be a boy. Before, she used to pull at – you know the sort of skin you

249

have – to make it sort of longer. Used to think I had an ugly cunt you see, I don't now. Free and easy.

Made me what I am.

The ideal woman, a kind of faithful slave, who administers without a word of complaint and certainly no payment, who speaks only when spoken to and is a jolly good chap. But a revolution is on the way, all over the country young girls are starting and shaking and if they terrify you they mean to is what she'd soon be saying out loud on the radio herself, you know.

One day a group of students was staging a protest outside a building. A BBC man came up with a mike. He chose the pretty girl. She was in a duffel coat strewing rose petals on the paving in front of the building.

What's a pretty girl like you doing at this sort of event?

She told him. This building is a real stinker. We're protesting it. We're mourning the death of architectural beauty.

But I've heard that this building is thought to be very efficient inside, he said.

We are outside, she said.

High in confidence. Low in confidence. Moodswings. Not a cosy girl. Don't come and see me today. Goodbye Cruel World, I'm off to join the circus. That was a pop song, Ken used it in his film when he followed her and three of the boys about and showed their lives, their work, their day. She filmed a dream instead, a real recurring dream (her final year dissertation was dreams) and after that film by Ken, in came all the dream jobs, the acting offers, 1963, dream of a year, *anus* mirabilis ha ha ha. All the things that had happened were the kind of thing, she supposed, that if they were ever to do one of those timelines of your life, born 6 March 1938, died whenever, would look sort of marvellous on a timeline. Grabowski show, radio work, married Clive, dancer on Ready Steady Go!, acting at Royal Court (acting was a time thing, though, sort of confidence trick. Painting was the real thing).

And then the future.

All the thirties up to thirty nine sounded great.

Between forty and fifty would be hell.

She hoped she'd never get hard. She'd never want to be too fixed in her ways.

(She'd be sketching and painting right up to her death. She'd sketch, among others, her friends in the band, 19th Nervous Breakdown. Paint it, Black. Her baby'd be in a cot at the foot of the bed. Her pictures after she died? Gone, lost, and the ones that weren't lost, thirty years in silence in her father's attic and an outhouse on her brother's farm, close shaves when it came to trips to the skip. The writer and curator who'd search for them thirty years after and find them in that outhouse? He'd burst into tears when he did.)

251

There was a circle of roses at the heart of her surname, all round the O in a woven open wreath.

There was a carved mermaid holding up the table.

There was never any money.

There was the brass bed, the paraffin stove.

There was pretending to be off-your-head berserk when the landlord came round hammering at the door to try to get to sleep with you.

There was wearing your coat all day in your room on the cold days.

None of that was life.

Life? was what you worked to catch, the intense happiness of an object slightly set apart from you. Painting? was what you did, alone, and you sat there, and it was your own terrible fight or your own lovely bit, but it was really terribly alone.

To take the moment before something had actually happened, and you didn't know if it was going to be terrible or if it might be very funny, something extraordinary actually happening and yet everybody around it not taking any notice at all.

She pasted. She cut. She painted. She concentrated.

In her dream, she slapped the past in its face.

Telling her schoolfriend Beryl, they were both sixteen, I'm going to be an artist.

Women don't get to be that, Beryl said.

I will. A serious artist. I want to be a painter.

It is yet another day, weather, time, news, stuff happening all across the country/countries, etc. Elisabeth goes for a walk in the village. Almost nobody is about. The few people out cutting things back in their gardens scowl at her or ignore her.

She steps to one side to make room on the narrow pavement and says hello to an old lady she passes.

The old lady nods, doesn't smile, walks past, imperious.

She comes to the spraypainted house. Either the people who were living here have moved or they've repainted the front of their house this bright seaside blue. It's like nothing's ever happened, unless you know to look a little more closely to make out the outline of the word HOME under the layer of blue.

When she gets back to her mother's the front

door is wide open. Her mother's friend Zoe comes out of it at a gallop. She almost collides with Elisabeth. In the near-miss she catches her up in her arms and swings her round in something like a Scottish country dance move, then skips backwards away from her down the path.

You'll never believe what your mother's gone and done, Zoe says.

She is laughing so much that Elisabeth can't not laugh too.

She got herself arrested. She threw a barometer at the fence, Zoe says.

What? Elisabeth says.

You know, Zoe says. Thing that measures pressure.

I know what a barometer is, Elisabeth says.

We were in the next village along, in the antiques place, you know it? Your mother took me there to show off how much she knows about antiques. And she saw a barometer she liked, so she bought it, cost a fair bit too. And we were on our way back in the car and the radio was on, and the news story came on about our new government cutting their funding for the houses where the kids who arrive here as asylum seekers have been staying, and the report said those kids are now going to be dumped in the same high-security places they put everybody. And your mother lost it. She started shouting about how those places are worse than jail, everyone under guard, bars on the windows, not fit for anybody, doubly not fit for kids. And then the next news story on the radio was the scrapping of the Minister for Refugees. She made me stop the car. She left the car door hanging open and she ran off up a path. So I got out and locked the car up and I followed her, and when I found her, well, I heard her before I saw her, she was shouting at men in a van at the fence, I mean fences, and she was shaking the barometer in the air at them and then I swear she threw it at the fence! And the fence gave this great cracking sound, a flash came off it, and the men went crazy because she'd shorted their fence. I couldn't help it. I yelled too. I yelled that's the way Wendy! That's the spirit!

Zoe tells Elisabeth that her mother'd been held for an hour, got off with a caution and is right now at the antiques yard down the road at the junction, stockpiling more stuff to throw at the fence, that her mother's new plan is that every day she's going to go and get herself arrested (and here she imitates Elisabeth's mother perfectly) *bombarding that fence with people's histories and with the artefacts of less cruel and more philanthropic times.*

She sent me home to bring the car, Zoe says. She's going to load it up with junk missiles. Oh, and I mustn't forget. They phoned for you on the house phone. Ten minutes ago.

Who did? Elisabeth says.

The hospital. Not hospital, the care place. Care providers.

Her mother's friend sees her face change. She stops being flippant immediately.

They said to tell you, she says. Your grandfather's been asking for you.

This time, the woman at reception doesn't even glance up. She is watching someone get garrotted on Game of Thrones on her iPad.

But then she says, still without looking up,

he's eaten a good lunch today, enough for like three people. Well, older people. We told him you'd be delighted he'd woken up and he said, please let my granddaughter know I'm looking forward to seeing her.

Elisabeth walks down the corridor, comes to his door and looks in.

He is asleep again.

She gets the chair from the corridor. She puts it beside the bed. She sits down. She gets out A Tale of Two Cities.

She closes her eyes. When she opens them

again his eyes are open. He is looking straight at her.

Hello again, Mr Gluck, she says.

Oh, hello, he says. Thought it'd be you. Good. Nice to see you. What you reading?

November again. It's more winter than autumn. That's not mist. It's fog.

The sycamore seeds hit the glass in the wind like – no, not like anything else, like sycamore seeds hitting window glass.

There've been a couple of windy nights. The leaves are stuck to the ground with the wet. The ones on the paving are yellow and rotting, wanwood, leafmeal. One is so stuck that when it eventually peels away, its leafshape left behind, shadow of a leaf, will last on the pavement till next spring.

The furniture in the garden is rusting. They've forgotten to put it away for the winter.

The trees are revealing their structures. There's the catch of fire in the air. All the souls are out

marauding. But there are roses, there are still roses.
In the damp and the cold, on a bush that looks
done, there's a wide-open rose, still.

Look at the colour of it.

I'm deeply indebted to everyone who's written about Pauline Boty but above all to the seminal work of Sue Tate and to her two volumes, Pauline Boty: Pop Artist and Woman (2013) and, as Sue Watling, with David Alan Mellor, Pauline Boty: The Only Blonde in the World (1998); and also to the interview with Boty by Nell Dunn in Vogue, September 1964, the full-length version of which is published in Nell Dunn's Talking to Women (1965). The stories about Christine Keeler which feature briefly in the novel can be found in Nothing But . . ., by Christine Keeler with Sandy Fawkes (1983), and Secrets and Lies, by Christine Keeler with Douglas Thompson (2012). I'm also fortunate to have been able to read a typescript of Sybille Bedford's as yet unpublished account of Stephen Ward's trial in 1963, The Worst We Can Do: A Concise Account of the Trial of Dr Stephen Ward, some of whose details of the trial (the court transcriptions of which still haven't been released into the public domain) have slipped into this novel.

Thank you, Simon, Anna, Hermione, Lesley B., Lesley L., Ellie, Sarah, and everyone at Hamish Hamilton.

Thank you, Andrew and Tracy
and everyone at Wylie's.

Thank you, Bridget Smith, Kate Thomson,
Neil MacPherson and Rachel Gatiss.

Thank you, Xandra. Thank you, Mary.

Thank you, Jackie.

Thank you, Sarah.

THE FIRST PERSON AND OTHER STORIES

From the Whitbread Award–winning author of *The Accidental* and *Hotel World* comes this stunning collection of stories set in a world of everyday dislocation, where people nevertheless find connection, mystery, and love. These tales are of ordinary but poignant beauty: at the pub, strangers regale each other with memories of Christmases past; lovers share tales over dinner about how they met their former lovers and each other; a woman tells a story to her fourteen-year-old self. As Smith explores the subtle links between what we know and what we feel, she creates an exuberant, masterly collection that is packed full of ideas, humor, nuance, and compassion. Ali Smith and the short story are made for each other.

Fiction

PUBLIC LIBRARY AND OTHER STORIES

Why are books so very powerful? What do the books we've read over our lives—our own personal libraries—make of us? What does the unraveling of our tradition of public libraries, so hard-won but now in jeopardy, say about us? The stories in Ali Smith's new collection are about what we do with books and what they do with us: how they travel with us; how they shock us, change us, challenge us, banish time while making us older, wiser, and ageless all at once; how they remind us to pay attention to the world we make. Woven between the stories are conversations with writers and readers reflecting on the essential role that libraries have played in their lives. At a time when public libraries around the world face threats of cuts and closures, this collection stands as a work of literary activism—and as a wonderful read from one of our finest authors.

Fiction

HOTEL WORLD

Five people: four are living; three are strangers; two are sisters; one, a teenage hotel chambermaid, has fallen to her death in a dumbwaiter. But her spirit lingers in the world, straining to recall things she never knew. And one night, all five women find themselves in the smooth plush environs of the Global Hotel, where the intersection of their very different fates makes up this playful, defiant, and richly inventive novel. Forget room service: this is a riotous elegy, a deadpan celebration of colliding worlds, and a spirited defense of love. Blending incisive wit with surprising compassion, *Hotel World* is a wonderfully invigorating, life-affirming book.

Fiction

HOW TO BE BOTH

Passionate, compassionate, vitally inventive, and scrupulously playful, Ali Smith's novels are like nothing else. Borrowing from painting's fresco technique to make an original literary double-take, *How to be both* is a novel all about art's versatility. It's a fast-moving, genre-bending conversation among forms, times, truths, and fictions. There's a Renaissance artist of the 1460s. There's the child of a child of the 1960s. Two tales of love and injustice twist into a singular yarn where time gets timeless, knowing gets mysterious, fictional gets real—and all life's givens get given a second chance.

Fiction

ALSO AVAILABLE

There but for the
The whole story and other stories

ANCHOR BOOKS
Available wherever books are sold.
www.anchorbooks.com